D0505376

Homecoming QUEEN

WINIFRED MADISON

SCHOLASTIC INC.

New York Toronto London Auckland Sydney Tokyo

Cover photograph by **Owen Brown**

ISBN 0-590-33488-3

12 11 10 9 8 7 6 5   4 5 6 7 8 9/8

Printed in the U.S.A.   06

Homecoming QUEEN

A Wildfire Book

WILDFIRE TITLES FROM SCHOLASTIC

Love Comes to Anne by Lucille S. Warner
I'm Christy by Maud Johnson
Beautiful Girl by Elisabeth Ogilvie
Superflirt by Helen Cavanagh
Dreams Can Come True by Jane Claypool Miner
I've Got a Crush on You by Carol Stanley
An April Love Story by Caroline B. Cooney
Dance with Me by Winifred Madison
Yours Truly, Love, Janie by Ann Reit
The Summer of the Sky-Blue Bikini by Jill Ross Klevin
The Best of Friends by Jill Ross Klevin
The Voices of Julie by Joan Oppenheimer
Second Best by Helen Cavanagh
A Place for Me by Helen Cavanagh
Sixteen Can Be Sweet by Maud Johnson
Take Care of My Girl by Carol Stanley
Lisa by Arlene Hale
Secret Love by Barbara Steiner
Nancy & Nick by Caroline B. Cooney
Wildfire Double Romance by Diane McClure Jones
Senior Class by Jane Claypool Miner
Cindy by Deborah Kent
Too Young to Know by Elisabeth Ogilvie
Junior Prom by Patricia Aks
Saturday Night Date by Maud Johnson
He Loves Me Not by Caroline Cooney
Good-bye, Pretty One by Lucille S. Warner
Just a Summer Girl by Helen Cavanagh
The Impossible Love by Arlene Hale
Sing About Us by Winifred Madison
The Searching Heart by Barbara Steiner
Write Every Day by Janet Quin-Harkin
Christy's Choice by Maud Johnson
The Wrong Boy by Carol Stanley
Make A Wish by Nancy Smiler Levinson
The Boy For Me by Jane Claypool Miner
Class Ring by Josephine Wunsch
Phone Calls by Ann Reit
Just You and Me by Ann Martin
Homecoming Queen by Winifred Madison

O^{ne}

On Friday, November 17, school let out at one o'clock because of the Homecoming Game. Laurie Hudson, surrounded by the other girls in the rest room, found it hard to keep from smiling at her reflection in the mirror. She didn't want to look too proud of herself or even too happy. Laurie knew this was something she had to watch, because not everyone was as lucky as she, and it would have been natural for some girls to resent her.

Yet it had never been more difficult to suppress her excitement. Last night at a huge, noisy rally, she had been elected Homecoming Queen. The crowds had cheered and cheered, and they would cheer again later that day when she would be presented with the crown by last year's queen. Her boyfriend Bob Hamilton, captain of the football team, had been chosen as king. Naturally they would share in the festivities later that day and at night at the dance after the game. What more could a girl want?

The room echoed with shouts and laughter, typical at the release from school and the promise of the weekend. Yet a few girls groaned, or complained of one thing or another, or remained significantly silent. *It's sad*, Laurie thought. Some were to face a lonely weekend, possibly sitting in front of a television set or, if they dared to go to the dance, risking an evening of loneliness while they watched others have fun. Laurie felt sorry for them, yet relieved that she had escaped such misery. Combing her thick, dark auburn hair she pretended that, as Homecoming Queen, she was queen of the school. *If only I were I'd do something for these poor, lonely girls* — but what? Then the moment's concern for them vanished and the exhilaration come back to her.

"Laurie, how can you be so calm when everything is so exciting?" a girl said, shoving in beside her.

"If it was me, I couldn't stand it!" Francie Holmes cried.

"Hey, I wish I was you for just one night. Tonight. How about changing places with me?" Laurie laughed sympathetically with Angela, all 158 pounds of her, as she snapped her gum defiantly and made jokes about herself. Her mouth turned up as though she had painted on a smile like a clown, but Laurie could see through it to the downward curve of misery. Why was it that now, of all times, she should become so sharply aware of the sadness in others when she had never been so thrilled with her life?

"If Bob agrees, I'll change places with you," Laurie said lightly, careful to keep pity or ridicule out of her voice, anything that would have hurt Angie's feelings. Of course the idea itself could not have been sillier.

"Thanks a million. Maybe not tonight but some other time, okay? You're so lucky, Laurie. What I wouldn't give to go out with Bob! If he even looked at me, I'd faint. . . ."

"Bob likes you a lot," Laurie lied. "He says you have a great sense of humor. You come off with some great lines."

"Did he really say that?" Angie asked eagerly.

"Sure."

You're always trying to make people feel good, Laurie mused to herself. This philosophy that Bob had pounded into Laurie came from his father, whose methods had shocked her. "It's not because you have to love somebody or go around feeling charitable; you just can't tell when someone can come in handy," Bob had said. And so Bob, like his father, smiled a great deal and made a habit of appearing the nicest, friendliest guy in the world. That was how Bob's father had gotten ahead and how Bob became popular.

Laurie, however, really wished she could

make Angie feel better about herself. It couldn't be easy to be so heavy and, of course, not witty in the least. Since everything was turning out so well for Laurie, it seemed the least she could do was to help others. If only she knew how! But she didn't dwell on it, for *she* was happy.

Lucky Laurie! Clearly she would never be as beautiful as Sondra Goodman, whose long blond hair and perfect features promised that she would become a highly successful model. Nor was she as bright as Phyllis Babbitt, who had been offered scholarships to three outstanding colleges. Nor was she talented like Charlotte Kane, the pianist who had already enjoyed three professional engagements. But Laurie had Bob, her boyfriend since fourth grade, the most popular person in the school. Surely the best athlete. No wonder he had been elected captain of the football team and would be Homecoming King, standing beside her during the ceremonies.

"Oh, Laurie, you must be perfectly happy. Perfectly!"

This last came from Tina Ball, a laughing blond who wriggled her way up through the crowd to the mirror so she could stand beside Laurie. Was there a hint of resentment in the remark? Tina had wanted ever so much to be Homecoming Queen.

"I am. Aren't you excited about the game?" Laurie said, changing the subject tactfully.

Bob was waiting for her in the hall. "At last! Took you ages in there."

"Sorry, Bob. The place was crowded. It's a big day."

She put her hand in his as they made their way through the crowded hall. "Nervous about the game?"

He grinned confidently. "Got it right here in the palm of my hand."

"Of course, darling. You're fantastic, and you'll win. You always do."

Was it not amazing, Laurie thought, that after all this time Bob still could overwhelm her with a certain Greek-godlike handsomeness! Tall, well-proportioned with naturally wide shoulders and slender hips, he measured up to the ideals of the classic male. The California sun had honeyed his smooth skin and bleached the thick, blond hair. Laurie loved everything about him, his bright, narrow blue eyes and full lips. He always dressed well, appearing at ease in the most expensive clothes, like the heavy, white Norwegian sweater he tossed over his shoulders. That night at the game he would run out on the field, with his helmet and the padded shoulders of his uniform, handsome as any warrior.

And she, the head cheerleader, would call the cheers with all her strength, wave her pom-poms, and go through the lively routine that she and the other girls had composed. How she would sing out! The whole crowd in the stadium would know that she must be in love to give herself so fully.

"Got your dress for tonight, Laurie?" Bob asked.

"Don't tell anyone. I bought it last week."

"Before you even knew if you'd be queen or not? What confidence!"

Laurie nodded, giggling. "I know. It was nervy, but only the best things are going to happen to us, right? Right. You're going to win tonight, too. We're winners, you and I. Bob, it's great, isn't it, such an honor!"

"Yeah, I guess, something like that," he said, chewing his gum thoughtfully.

As they passed the principal's office on their way out of the school, they were held up by a jam of too many students wanting to get out all at once. Standing as they paused, they became aware of a girl sitting in the small waiting room. A new girl in school? Laurie found her pretty enough without being extraordinary. Lovely hair, Laurie thought, not unlike her own, curling down to her shoulders, but whereas Laurie's tended to be dark, this girl's, a much lighter auburn, made a halo around her head. But it was her smile that made her spectacular, a wide, inviting grin that she flashed at Bob with only a passing glance at Laurie.

"Who is that girl? Do we know her?" Bob asked.

"Never saw her before. I thought I knew everyone here."

"She smiles as if she knows us," Bob said, smiling back. "Maybe she's just a friendly type."

A little too friendly, Laurie thought, but said jokingly, "Well, darling, you're so famous, captain of the team, Homecoming King and all that, of course she knows you. Maybe we should become really royal, lifting our hands with that Queen Elizabeth wave."

Bob laughed as Laurie took on the exaggerated, smug expression of a queen passing by in her Rolls-Royce. It always surprised Bob when Laurie imitated personalities, good-naturedly poking fun at them, although she was careful only to chose public figures, never anyone from school.

At last the bottleneck cleared and Laurie shivered as she and Bob found themselves out in the raw November wind.

"Want to come over to my house for lunch, Bob?"

"No thanks, Laurie. I'm allowing myself only one steak and my father wants to take me out for it. Gotta meet him in ten minutes. And then . . . afternoon before the game. You know what that means. I'll see you on the field. You know, Laurie, I'm really proud of you. You're one fantastic cheerleader. It always amazes me you've got so much zip."

"It's all for you, Bob. A hero like you. So there!"

She punched him playfully, lightly. He caught her hand, bent down, and kissed her. It was not the romantic kiss Laurie wanted, but a more affectionate, assured kiss, as if he didn't have the time to woo her. An unwelcome thought, she brushed it aside. Naturally his mind was on the big game.

"See you later, Laurie. At the game."

"I'l be proud of you, Bob. Real proud."

She put her hands in his, reassured by the large, affectionate squeeze. Now she knew, positively, that their understanding was so deep that nothing could ever come between them.

"See you later, darling."

Another kiss, a brief one for good luck. And then, because they both had to hurry, they separated. Laurie, pulling her bulky sweater around her to ward off the chill of the day, moved briskly. There was so much to do — so much before the magic night!

Two

The day moved in strange rhythms, now fast, now slow. Mrs. Hudson had taken the afternoon off from her work because Laurie's new dress — masses of white lace with a square cut neckline and intricate puffed sleeves — needed to be taken it at the waist and rehemmed.

Unable to eat any lunch, Laurie tried on the dress and stood patiently in her bedroom while her mother kneeled on a cushion, her mouth filled with pins. Tracy, Laurie's ten-year-old sister, sat cross-legged on the bed and watched.

"Oh! I wish I was you, Laurie! I wish Bob was my boyfriend and I was Homecoming Queen. You have all the luck."

"Not all of it," Laurie said. "Someday you'll go to high school, you'll become very popular, and there'll be somebody else just as nice as Bob. And you'll go to all the dances, I'll bet."

"But I can't wait that long!" she whined, a tiny figure in jeans and T-shirt. *Once I was like that*, Laurie thought wistfully, *thinking the future would never come.*

"That waistline of yours . . . mmm! Once mine was tiny like that. Hold still, Laurie. I want to get it right," Mrs. Hudson said.

"It's such a beautiful dress," Laurie said.

"And it cost so much!" Tracy piped up.

"I know. Mom, I know it was too much, but I'll work and pay for it. Really. It's just that I had to have it."

"Don't worry about it. Of course you had to have it now. It's not every day you get to be Homecoming Queen. And it is lovely, the way it floats. Why, you could almost be a bride in a dress like this."

A bride! Laurie caught her breath. If being Homecoming Queen could be compared to a mountain peak, why, marriage was an even higher peak. The very thought of it could make her dizzy, although she and Bob had planned it for years and years, or so it seemed. The future lay ahead in a hazy glow.

"Mom, don't talk about being a bride yet!" Laurie said, as if talking of one's future would tempt bad luck. This very day was turning out to be so exciting she never wanted it to end, could not even think about the next day.

"Okay, Queen, let me see how it falls. Turn around slowly now."

Laurie turned slowly but rose on her tiptoes, as if dancing, and Tracy let out a long sigh of such yearning that Mrs. Hudson hugged her. "Poor Tracy! Please don't grow up too soon. And now we'd better go and let Laurie take a nap. Yes, Laurie, I insist. You're going to have an exhausting night, and you need it. I wish you'd have something to eat."

"Mom, I can't. I'm full of butterflies. I can't be much of a cheerleader if I'm full of your stew. Anyway, we're having a party at Bob's house after the dance, and you know the kind of buffet Mrs. Hamilton puts out. So you don't have to worry about your daughter starving."

"It's the last thing I'd really worry about. But the drinking . . ."

"I avoid it. Honest. But that crowd — well, it's one thing I don't like about them. But I don't know what I can do about it."

"Do they get sick? Yuck," Tracy said, making illustrative sounds.

"Don't be disgusting, Tracy," Laurie said. "But sometimes they get sick. Or they fight, or get silly, or throw someone in the swimming pool. But if I go with Bob and those are our friends, I'd better get used to it. Right?"

Mrs. Hudson pursed her lips, then relaxed. "Well, you take care of yourself, Laurie Hudson. Bob doesn't drink too much, does he, Laurie?"

"Mom! You're so straitlaced. Look, you've brought me up well and you don't have to worry. I mean it. Bob drinks a little but even when he drinks, he only becomes a little quiet. You know?"

Quiet was a polite word for sullen, a soft word for the silences Bob sometimes sank into. Bob's father drank too much. . . .

"I know what you're thinking, Mom, and you don't have to worry. Even when Bob drinks, he sees that our relationship is . . . ahem . . . pure, because I want it that way. And now I don't want to talk about it anymore because this is the most perfect day I've ever had."

"Of course. Tracy, let Laurie take a nap."

Mrs. Hudson closed the drapes in Laurie's room and covered her with a quilt, for the wind rattling against the thinly insulated walls made the bedroom drafty and cold. And then Laurie was alone. And unable to sleep.

If everything is so perfect, she wondered, what was this tiny doubt that clawed her softly but definitely, putting her on edge. Maybe it's just nervousness, she decided, yet a tiny voice, just below the level of her conscious mind, whispered, *Watch out, Laurie, watch out*.

"Of course it's nerves," she said, dismissing the unpleasant thought. After all, becoming a queen was hardly an everyday event, and besides, the warning made no sense.

It made more sense to review what would happen, to picture herself as she would appear in a few hours, jumping and shouting and taking part in the energetic routine she had worked up with the other pom-pom girls. The lights would come on brighter than day, and the bands would blare. And then that thrilling moment when the team would run out on the field. For a moment Bob's eyes would meet hers, and she would whisper the word he needed to hear. "Win!" His eyes would flash, and then the game would begin, and now as before, almost without fail, he would play brilliantly. If he was a hero, he deserved it. Laurie would concentrate tonight, as at every other game, on his winning, on his playing better than anyone else, on his becoming the champion.

Tonight they would be crowned. After the game they would shower and dress, and then go to the dance with its festivities, a very special dance. Like a fairy-tale ball. And after that the party at the Hamiltons'. And after that?

She didn't know, couldn't tell. She would be with Bob. It was all that mattered.

Then Laurie fell asleep, for it was already dusk when her mother woke her, bringing her a bowl of tomato soup and a tiny roll.

Laurie took a bath, a long, soapy bath; she got into the short, swingy blue skirt, the white boots, and the white sweater with its big blue letter. Tracy watched.

"Hey, Laurie, is this the last game?"

"Almost," Laurie said soberly, realizing that in a few weeks it would all be over. But one mustn't think of endings, she told herself, only of something glorious. Like this day. Her day.

She heard the sound of the band as she approached the school and from that point on, the excitement mounted. She felt higher and higher. Never had she cheered with so much spirit. Never had the team running out on the field seemed more gracefully masculine and so determined to win as they did that night. The crowds cheered. For a while the balance of the game held uncertainly. And then with a valiant effort the Edgewood team won!

Bob was carried around the field on the shoulders of the team. Photographers appeared and reappeared, taking pictures. The drums beat a tattoo again and again and still again.

And then she had to go home to change. Bob would be calling for her soon.

Her father hugged her. A sports buff, he said he was supposed to be working that night in the hardware store, but he wouldn't have missed the game for anything, even if it meant working late the next week.

"And I'm so proud of you, Laurie!"

"All right, then," Mrs. Hudson said. "Let her go so she can get dressed for the dance."

Laurie showered, then carefully put on the makeup she had bought and stepped back to admire the effect. That, too, had been costly, but the girls in the Gang could always tell good makeup and raised their eyebrows at the cheap stuff most of the girls at Edgewood High wore. Laurie had decided that on this night nothing but the best would do. At the same time, her own color was so high with excitement that the makeup hardly made any difference.

Her mother helped her put on the dress. Then panic set in. Where were her shoes? She tore through the closet and could not find them. It was Mrs. Hudson who saw Tracy stomping around in them.

Everything was rushing like an old movie, when the characters move too stiffly and too fast. Laurie was brushing her hair as the doorbell rang, and then Bob was waiting in the living room — so handsome that Laurie caught her breath. She touched the bruise on his cheek with tender fingers, as if it only made him all the more heroic.

"Hey, you're gorgeous!" he said. "Wow!"

But he was in a hurry to be off, though her father insisted on discussing the game with Bob. Now Tracy clung to him, and Mrs. Hudson appeared with her camera.

"I've got to get your pictures," she said. "Now, Bob, if you'll stand with Laurie. And Laurie, one alone of you. And now . . ."

"Oh, Mother," Laurie groaned as the tiny flashbulbs went off as she and Bob posed, pretending at one point to be dancing together.

Finally the last good-byes were said, the final warnings to be careful in the car, not drink too much, behave, and "be sure to have a good time."

"Etcetera!" Laurie groaned as she and Bob stepped out into the chilly November night.

She drew the shawl her mother had crocheted around her shoulder. While her quilted down jacket would have been warmer, and her mother had advised her to take it, Laurie would rather have frozen than put it over her lovely white dress. She shivered only a little as she hurried with Bob toward the white Mercedes his father had let him take for the evening. The king and queen going to the ball!

"Happy?" Laurie asked Bob.

"Sure. We smashed 'em, didn't we? What a game! And now . . . you look terrific. Pretty dress."

"Thanks. You're pretty handsome yourself," Laurie said as he opened the door of the car for her. He talked about the game all the way to the dance, and she thought of how when they arrived at the gym the spotlights would center on them. The crowds would cheer and this would be the most beautiful moment of her life.

Three

The next day Laurie awoke at noon. As usual, her fingers felt for the tiny gold football that hung from a chain around her neck. A nervous habit, touching this precious football from Bob, as though she were touching Bob's love.

But she did not linger, for her stomach was sending her urgent messages, driving her quickly to the bathroom, where she got sick. She glanced in the mirror to see a pale, pasty-faced queen if ever there was one, then crawled back to bed with a stinging headache. She had not planned to drink, and all she had had were two glasses of punch at the Hamiltons'. Bob had given it to her, swearing it was pure fruit juice. It was not a nice trick, but he had only wanted to make her even happier than she already was.

Mrs. Hudson looked in on Laurie. "How was the big night? Tired, are you? Just for today, today only, I'll treat you to breakfast in bed. How about some poached eggs?"

"Please . . . don't mention food. I'm turning green."

"Black coffee then? Oh, Laurie, I thought you weren't going to drink."

"I wasn't. I'll explain later."

Laurie was still thinking of herself as the luckiest girl in the world, but she would have been luckier without the hangover.

"Well, I'll bring you a pot of black coffee, and you can drink it whenever you want."

"Thanks, Mom. I know I'm supposed to clean house today. Maybe in a little while, okay?"

"Don't worry about it. Did you have a wonderful night?"

"Sure, Mom, it was fabulous. Everything I'd ever dreamed about."

But was that true? Everything had gone well enough, and yet something was missing. Laurie tried to find what the missing piece could be, but like a jigsaw puzzle lacking the one key part, it didn't quite come together. Everything had gone pretty much as she had expected, as though they had rehearsed it for a long, long time. Yet it lacked spontaneity. *So what did you expect, Laurie? You can't make a blue-*

print for something and then expect it to be fresh and inventive at the last minute. The important thing was to appear happy, thoroughly happy.

Ten minutes later Mrs. Hudson and Tracy appeared.

"Are you feeling any better? Tell me all about the evening, quick, because I've got to get to work. How did it go?"

"It was beautiful and exciting, couldn't have been better."

"And?"

"It was the way we thought it would be. The presentation and ceremonies, which were kind of exciting, then we danced and afterward the Gang went over to the Hamiltons'. What a spread! Lobster salad and a cake shaped like a football, all chocolate and creamy . . . you would have loved it."

"You'll have to describe all that later. Then what?"

"At about one-thirty or two, we all got into cars and rode down to the beach."

She would leave out the part about the racing, the crazy, reckless driving, the way she had clung to Bob and shut her eyes, really frightened.

"Laurie, were they racing?"

"Only a little. Well, we got to the beach, and Bob and I went for a walk in the moonlight. It was chilly but beautiful. We sat on the rocks."

"And what happened?" Tracy asked, eyes wide as she waited for romantic details.

"You look just like Patch when someone puts out meat for him. He can't wait to pounce on it. Sorry, Tracy, some things are private."

Tracy stuck out her tongue.

"Are you sure you don't have a little more to tell us?" Mrs. Hudson asked. Laurie knew well enough what was on her mind.

"Mom, don't push! When it's time for me to tell you something, I will. Oh . . . Mother!"

"All right, don't get upset. I just wondered, that's all."

"There's nothing to tell. Everyone got hungry, and we went to Morley's for breakfast. I was home by six-thirty this morning."

"What's it like at Morley's?" Tracy had to know, and Laurie couldn't blame her. Morley's, a castlelike restaurant overlooking the ocean, had served a breakfast in their exclusive garden court.

"I'd love to know, too," Mrs. Hudson said, "but I've got to get to work. Save it for when I get home. Come on, Tracy. Tracy!"

But she had disappeared with Laurie's tiara and was posing in front of the mirror, as if she were the one who had been crowned. Mrs. Hudson made her put it back and persuaded her to spend the rest of the afternoon at a friend's house, so that Laurie could sleep off the excitement of the last few days.

"Thanks, Mom, you're a doll."

"Just for today, darling. Remember, you may be queen but I'm the queen mother. So get well!"

Mrs. Hudson plugged in the percolator, kissed her daughter, and left.

Laurie sighed, glad to be alone at last.

No longer ill, but somehow weary, Laurie needed a long, quiet time. Half-asleep, half-awake, she let the images come and go.

On a sun-dappled day in July when she was nine, she had gone to the supermarket for her mother. For nearly two years now they had lived in East Edgewood in a slightly rundown tract home that closely resembled the other ninety-nine tract homes clustered there, each with a tiny lawn in front, a spindly street tree, and a minuscule patio in back. On the dry, hot summer days, Laurie dreamed of escaping, and so did not really mind when her mother sent her to the store in an older tree-shaded section of Edgewood where spacious houses from an earlier time spread over ample lawns.

On that day in July as she walked home slowly, lingering under the shade of a spreading oak, something light hit her on the head. A cookie! Looking up, she saw a tow-headed boy grinning from his position on a high, sturdy limb.

"Hi! Wanna go swimming?" he asked.

"Where?"

"We got a pool out back. C'mon."

"I haven't got a bathing suit with me."

"Well, you can sit and watch me swim then. I'll show you how I dive."

He jumped down neatly from one limb to another and landed gracefully before her. She walked with him across the shaded lawn, through the wide veranda of a rambling white house, and out toward the back where a turquoise blue pool nestled in a garden. A kind of heaven, it astounded Laurie, for it was so close to East Edgewood. And yet so very different!

"I'm Bob Hamilton. I've never seen you before. Who are you?"

"Laurie Hudson. I haven't seen you either."

"Course not. We just moved here a week ago."

"C'mon," he said as Laurie, shy, hung back. She sat down beside the pool, a small, large-eyed child in shorts and a T-shirt. She knew she should get home soon with the groceries, for the milk would sour in the summer heat. Still, she sat mesmerized as Bob dropped his khaki shorts to reveal his swimming trunks and dove into the pool, going down deep and then coming up, swimming swiftly to the far end of the pool and back, then scrambling out. Though Laurie knew nothing about swimming, she thought he must be very good.

"Didja watch me dive?" he asked.

"Oh, yes. It was real good," Laurie said, with genuine admiration.

"Okay, watch this!" he cried out, and she

watched him perform a jackknife dive, then a dive in which he turned a somersault; then he said he must do it again better, and then still more dives. Laurie had sat entranced, and her eyes had never left him.

"Hey, Mom, this is Laurie," he said as a pretty blond woman, very slender and poised, came toward the pool with a tray of lemonade and cookies in her hands. "She likes to watch me dive."

Laurie, the sixteen-year-old Laurie, sat up in bed remembering the scene and said to herself, *That's really what he wanted, someone to watch him.*

At that time Mrs. Hamilton had about her a certain air, which Laurie would later recognize as rich, although she wasn't sure exactly what that quality was. When Strawberry Hill was built, many of the women who lived in the new, exclusive modern homes moved and talked like Mrs. Hamilton. A rich look — something that Mrs. Hudson, good-looking though she was, would never have.

"Do you live around here, Laurie?"

"Sort of, in East Edgewood."

"Oh, I see." A long pause which made Laurie uncomfortable, but then Mrs. Hamilton smiled warmly. "Isn't it nice that now Bob has someone to play with!"

At the time Laurie was excited about Bob and about being invited to the big house. Yet now the words sent a different message. She was not thought of as a person in her own right, but a nice, friendly companion for Bob.

And why should she think of that now when everything had turned out so well? Although Mrs. Hamilton had often regarded Laurie with a certain indefinable coldness and too-frequent suggestions that she have her hair "styled, not simply cut," or that she would do well to wear designer jeans rather than ordinary ones, she had been pleasant enough. "After all, you're Bob's girl!" she had once remarked.

"Is your father successful?" Bob had asked one day during that first summer. The question astounded her.

"I don't know what you mean."

"Let me explain it. My father's successful. He's going to be the biggest real-estate man in Edgewood. What does your father do?"

"He works in a hardware store," she said shyly. "He likes sports a lot."

"No kidding? That's great," Bob said, and so her father was somehow redeemed.

One night she met Bob's father, a tall man, well-tanned, with a soft drawl in his speech and an apparently easygoing manner. He smiled at Laurie and put his hand over her thatch of curly hair.

"I've gotta admit," he said, "Bob knows how to pick his girls."

She had blushed and giggled. Her life was changing, and she wondered what was coming next.

And so they became childhood sweethearts. It simply happened that way. There was never anyone else for Laurie all the way through school, and for Bob this also appeared to be so. In the first years that they knew each other they played together — climbing the big trees around the house, swimming, playing table tennis on the wide veranda.

At first she had been afraid to swim.

"Afraid? You admit you're afraid? Come on, I'll teach you."

So she had come over in her bathing suit, and he had taught her well, so that she not only overcame her fear but won his approval. "Not bad. You won't make the Olympics, but you can sure swim."

"Thanks," she had said gratefully. He encouraged her to dive, to swim many laps so she could do it without getting tired, but he never competed with her. Long after Laurie would finish her afternoon swim, she would lie at the edge of the pool and admire Bob, timing him with his stopwatch.

Admiring Bob seemed to be the role chosen for her, but she accepted it eagerly. She had never known anyone like him. And her parents liked him, too.

"That boy's gonna be a great athlete," her father, the sports enthusiast, predicted.

"And he seems so nice," her mother said. "But you watch out for him, Laurie Hudson. I think he's used to having his own way."

"Oh, *Mother*, how can you talk like that? We're just friends."

It wasn't until after the first junior high dance that something more happened. "I love you, Laurie," he had said.

"And I love you."

He had kissed her before, a boyish smack on the cheek from time to time, but this was a slow, rich kiss with his lips pressed fully against her own. On that night, when the stars sang in the deep autumn sky, they discovered that they were in love, and they dared to talk about it. They became the school lovers and were frequently kidded about it. But Bob had shrugged his shoulders — why keep it a secret?

Everything had gone well. Happy years! Laurie, awake now, let her eyes rest on the pale gold tiara which her mother had placed on the bureau. Getting out of bed she put it on her head, laughing at her crown because it contrasted so strangely with her flannel pajamas.

Still languid, she drew the water for a bath. Lying in it, she thought about Bob and her life with him.

Mr. Hamilton, determined to be the most successful real estate agent in Edgewood, had developed an area of homes for the wealthier residents of the small city. Soon the Hamiltons moved to a sprawling redwood house on Strawberry Hill, where luxurious homes lay half-hidden in the foliage of the mildly undulating landscape. Laurie feared that this change might affect her relationship with Bob, but Bob practically insisted that she come out every day. In fact, he lent her his old ten-speed to replace Laurie's awkward one-speed bicycle.

Gradually many of the boys who lived in Strawberry Hill hung around the Hamiltons', for Bob became known as the leading athlete in school, and they admired him. Then the girls who lived in that area or the other wealthier parts of town also wandered over to the Hamiltons'. Sally Howe, Jean Myers, Teri Grote, Valerie Smith . . . they all had that certain "society" quality Mrs. Hamilton possessed and Laurie did not. But what was it that made the difference?

Still, Laurie found that the girls liked her well enough from the very beginning. She knew that they often had parties and did things together which she was never invited to. But the Gang, made up of these frequent visitors to the Hamiltons', often had parties or picnics at the beach twenty miles away, and it was always taken for granted that Bob and Laurie would come together.

The other girls were charming, but Bob had always loved her. *How lucky I am!* Laurie thought as she soaped herself lazily. The tiny gold football caught the light as it dangled at the end of its chain.

And we never fought, Laurie said to herself, rinsing herself off, just as though she were relating the story to someone. Of course there was that time last year when she wanted to join the chorus, an outstanding musical organization at school, for she loved to sing. Bob did not object directly but spoke in a drawling, persuasive way that Laurie recognized as his father's.

"If you really want to, honey, go ahead. But Laurie, I love it so much when you come to football practice. Being a cheerleader takes you away from me too much as it is, and you know how demanding and tough it is to be on the team. And when you're there, sitting in the bleachers watchin' me, baby, that's when I know I'm gonna win. You're my good-luck piece, Laurie. You know that?"

And so she hadn't joined the chorus after all. When she wasn't practicing with the cheerleaders, she sat in the bleachers — a lone figure watching the team exercising, tackling, running, kicking the ball. So many long hours! More than once she began to walk away, but each time Bob chose to wave at her or yell "Hiya, honey," and so she stayed.

At the time, she supposed it was rather sweet that Bob seemed to depend on her, but now it occurred to Laurie that it was too bad to have missed out on the singing.

They did have one fight. Only one. During their junior year, a long-legged boy with dark hair and direct gray eyes had come to Edgewood. He had tried out for track and had immediately broken all the school records, including Bob's. Bob could hardly believe that he had been beaten. He entered a race with this newcomer, Gregory Munson, and lost. Bob withdrew from track.

"Who needs it? It takes long legs but no brain to speak of. Football requires some pretty foxy thinking."

"Sure, darling, and you're so great at football. And swimming. And just about everything. So why bother with track?"

Nevertheless, the defeat he suffered rankled him, and later in the year when the Gang decided to have a big party and invite all the good athletes in school — the swimmers, the football team, the basketball heroes, and everyone who had made a mark — Greg Munson's name was omitted.

"Bob, you've forgotten Greg. He's not like you, of course, but he's been making history around here, winning a lot of meets," Laurie had said.

"Track is not really a sport," Bob said, and for the first time Laurie thought him pompous.

"Of course it's a sport, Bob. Why else would they have it in the Olympics?"

Naturally Bob was aware of this, but he still smarted from having been beaten by Greg.

"Look, it won't hurt to invite him. You're so fantastic, you can afford to be generous," she coaxed him gently. But a dark suspicion changed his point of view.

"Hey, Laurie, how come you're so interested in Beanpole's feelings? Are you interested in him or something?"

"Don't be silly. I don't even know him.

We're in the same English class, but I don't know anything about him. I just think he should be invited, that's all."

Bob's mouth grew hard, as if someone had poured cement over it, and his eyes narrowed. He would not give in, and for the first time ever Laurie stood her ground stubbornly, then went home and cried for hours. At nine that night she and Bob phoned each other, dialing at the same time, each receiving busy signals. Laurie learned this fifteen minutes later when Bob showed up at the front door. Not wanting to talk in front of her parents and careful to avoid a conversation about sports with Mr. Hudson, Bob rushed Laurie out to the Dinky, a red Fiat, which his mother used to drive. He drove her to Samson's where they made up over a sundae.

"Laurie, honey, we've never had a fight, and I don't want one now. I couldn't bear it."

"Neither could I. Oh, Bob, I've been so miserable all day. See how red my eyes are from crying. I couldn't bear to lose you."

"And I don't want to lose you, certainly not over a goon like Munson."

"Bob, I don't think he's a goon at all, and that's that. But after all, it's your party, so do what you like, and I won't say another word."

He put his large, warm hands over hers, and they leaned forward to kiss over the strawberry sundae they were sharing. They laughed, relieved and embarrassed and, most of all, happy to be together again. Bob began to talk of the future.

It was a theme they had discussed before, improving on details until their plans were blueprinted. After graduation, Bob would go to a school of business administration, one that didn't require college, and Laurie would study accounting and typing, all those subjects that would make it possible for her to help Bob when he entered his father's business. They would marry, live in a small cottage out near the golf course, and later they would move to Strawberry Hill. As she thought of it, feelings of excitement coursed through Laurie's veins. Bob's eyes were shining.

"It means one thing, Laurie. You're interested in me and me alone. Nobody else. I couldn't stand it if I thought —"

"Bob, how can you even think such a thing? I care for you so much, nobody else exists, well, hardly."

"Good, keep it that way."

He had not mentioned anything about his remaining true to her, but she was so filled with dreams of their wonderful future, she could not imagine him becoming interested in another girl.

And though they kissed for a long time in the front seat of the Fiat — as if they would cling to each other forever — he respected her enough not to go too far. "It's because I really love you, Laurie. Maybe we ought to get married sooner."

"Maybe," she said, eyes glistening. But she could not answer to it that night. It was enough to sit there together loving each other until at last the lights flickered on and off in the house, and Laurie knew it was time to go in.

And so why, Laurie asked herself, as she got out of the tub and dried herself, *do I remember such things now of all times? And last night everything was so exciting, so very wonderful.*

She dressed and brushed her hair slowly. She had promised to clean the house today, and in a few minutes she'd begin. Later she would have to tell the family all about the dance, the compliments, the ceremonies, all the photographers wanting to take their pictures, and the way she and Bob had felt themselves the very center of everything.

And yet, what she could never tell anyone was a certain feeling of foreboding so minor she could not possibly have explained it, much less put it into words. It was only a sensation, like a warning buzz.

As she danced with Bob, she did as he did, that is, she smiled at everyone. Yet at the same time she was wondering whether two other people were there. Greg Munson? She couldn't find him. How odd that this should disappoint her when she hardly knew him, when they never spoke. Yet she would have liked it had he seen her in this beautiful dress and with the crown on her head.

This was more understandable than an irrational fear that she might see another person there. At first she couldn't remember who it might be, but halfway through the evening she recalled it was the girl who had sat in the principal's office that afternoon and smiled so intensively at Bob. It made no sense that Laurie should be relieved at her absence. She didn't even know her.

The party at the Hamiltons', lavish and exciting as always, brought up a different problem. Since Laurie was one of those individuals who react to alcohol by becoming ill and depressed, she never drank anything more powerful than ginger ale. Bob knew this, yet gave her a glass of the powerful punch his mother had made for the occasion. "C'mon, Laurie. Pure fruit juice!" he said.

"Bob, I think I'll skip it," she had answered lightly.

"Darn it, Laurie, it's time you grew up and learned to drink like everyone else. Come on, honey." Under the syrupy sweetness of his voice, Laurie heard the order, drink up or else. She hesitated.

"Are you one of us or aren't you? Maybe you think you're too good to drink with us. How do you think we like it when you set yourself up above everyone?"

"That's not it at all, Bob. You know it." She suspected that Bob was drunk but went on anyway. "Why should anyone care whether I drink or not? All right, Bob, if it makes you happy."

And so she took the glass, for she couldn't fight on that night in particular. She planned not to drink it, but he watched until she emptied the glass. Then he brought her another, but she managed to leave most of it, as Sally Howe and two members of the team came up to discuss a trip to the beach.

Laurie's parents must never know how frightened she had been as the cars raced, seven cars practically jostling each other, almost forcing Bob's car off the road at one point into a gully that lay below.

But the beach was never lovelier — or colder — as the moon showed itself fully and generously. Bob suggested that they take off their shoes and walk along the beach, a silly thing to do in evening clothes, but never had a night been more romantic. Tiny clouds scudded by, softening the hard, brilliant light of the moon. Laurie held her mother's thin woolen shawl tightly around her shoulders. Bob had had the foresight to bring along a car blanket.

"Let's sit on the rocks over there," he said, and so he helped her up to the top one and there they sat, the blanket wrapped around both of them, holding them together. The world had become strangely quiet except for the roar of the waves and an occasional burst of laughter from someone on the beach.

Bob put his arm around Laurie and pulled

her toward him. He kissed her, but something was missing, as though he was thinking of something else. She put her hand in his and snuggled close.

"Are you happy, Bob? It's been such a great triumph for you. The game was the best ever. I'm really proud of you."

"Thanks, Laurie."

"A lot of people say you should go in for sports, become a pro."

"Yeah? Is that what they're saying? I happen to know what I'm doing."

"That's really what counts," she said weakly. She expected that he would talk about the game or that he would sigh with the relief that usually follows a tense day, but he seemed to fall into a glum silence she could not understand.

"What are you thinking about, honey?" she asked lightly, afraid to ask the real questions on her lips. *Do you love me?* or *What's the matter?* She kept the tone of her voice light to hide the vague uneasiness that marred the romantic night. A headache from the punch began to torment her and was spoiling the mood of the evening.

"What am I thinkin' 'bout? Well, honey chile, I'm thinkin' of a big juicy steak. Aren't you hungry?"

"A little," she admitted, but it was something else she needed more than food. As if remembering there was something he ought to do, he kissed her; for a few moments his warm, full lips pressing against hers and his arms crushing her ribs reassured her that everything was going to be all right. She wanted him to say that he loved her, but he grinned, patted her hair, and kissed the tip of her nose as if she were a pet.

"Hey, let's wake everyone up and go git some breakfast," he said, and Laurie was startled. He took on an exaggerated Southern accent once in a while, for his mother had came from Virginia and prided herself on her Southern speech. But Bob only did it when he wanted to keep from saying what he actually felt. He and Laurie stepped carefully off the rocks, and then walked silently over the beach and back to the car where Bob blew the horn again and again, blasting the quiet of the night until everyone, furious with the jarring noise in the romantic night, came over. Everyone decided to go over to Morley's for breakfast.

Laurie, more hopeful now, looked forward to going to this well-known restaurant, built with a tower at one end. The noisy, disorderly crowd clattered across the floor. At last they were seated. Laurie, looking out of the window, saw the dawn coming up, fresh and new; in the face of it everyone seemed faded and worn, faces pale from lack of sleep or slightly ill from too much liquor, hair disheveled, beautiful gowns now wrinkled.

"Hey, you're supposed to be happy," Bob said in a fierce whisper as he waited for his steak.

"*Supposed* to be?" she retorted, thinking it was impossible to be happy because one was *supposed* to be. Yet she smiled as agreeably as she could. Perhaps she was becoming a party pooper, silent and, in spite of herself, disapproving.

The conversation around the table shifted to weekend plans. Bob turned to Laurie. "What's up?"

"We're going to a party at Linda Cahill's. Tomorrow . . . I mean, tonight."

Linda, not a member of the Gang, was Laurie's friend and also a neighbor. They knew each other and always planned to get together but seldom did. Linda had invited them to her party, and Bob had said okay. But now he frowned.

"Gee, hon, I can't make it. Forgot all about it actually. Tomorrow the family's going to Monterey to look at a new boat my father might get. Anyway, I could use a breather."

"Linda will be disappointed. She's really very nice."

"She'll get over the heartbreak," he said, and then someone at the table began to sing, and Bob joined in. *How drunk they sound,* Laurie thought.

At last the party broke up, and Bob took her home. He parked in front of the house and kissed her. "Tired, baby? It was a good show you put on."

"You were really the hero. Bob . . . I'll never forget it, will you?"

"Nope. Never," he said. They kissed lightly, too exhausted to give each other more than a warm embrace.

Laurie got out of the car and had staggered halfway up the walk, her shoes definitely pinching, when Bob called her back to the car.

"Hey, Laurie, you forgot your crown!"

"How could I forget!"

The tiara, lying in the backseat, appeared light and insubstantial in the early morning light. Bob handed it to her and she carried it loosely in her hand.

Laurie had just finished putting on jeans and a shirt when her mother and Tracy burst into the room, their arms filled with newspapers.

"Your pictures are all over!"

She squealed with excitement as she looked through the papers, seeing pictures of herself standing beside Bob, being crowned, laughing happily as they danced alone on the dance floor. Long articles emphasized Bob's brilliance as a football player and Laurie's enthusiasm as a cheerleader.

"Here's the nicest picture of all!" Mrs. Hudson said, and Laurie agreed.

There they were, she and Bob, standing close together and looking up as though they were facing a brilliant and beautiful future. Actually, they had been told simply to face the photographer, but the camera had caught something else — their hope and their love and the way it seemed right for them to be together.

Of course it's right, Laurie said to herself as she cut out the picture to put in her scrapbook.

Now she felt all right again. Good. Bursting with energy. All was well with her and Bob, all was well with the world.

and there we stayed right, right, reached be
Franklin

it we never speak Junior high. "He'll
as I prefer for one to bet I have never
Laurie. It isn't fair dear. I don't believe
with power. All. It's you will me
office would the me to

*F*our

"It feels like winter already!" Mrs. Hudson cried on Monday morning. Most likely it would never snow in Edgewood. Laurie had never even seen snow until those winter week-ends the Hamiltons took her to their cabin in the Sierras — *that* was winter. But in Edge-wood the color faded from the sky and the wind blew with a menacing chill as it ripped all those last clinging leaves from the trees.

"Mom, I may be home late this afternoon. Bob wants to begin swimming practice for an hour or so, because as soon as football is fin-ished he's joining the swim team. He wants me to time him."

"Laurie, I don't know why you have to give

up your time to watch Bob swim, but if that's how you want to spend your days, go right ahead."

"Just a minute," Mr. Hudson broke in, lifting his head from the sports page of the morning paper. "That boy is a fine athlete. Why, he could go as far as he wants, maybe the Olympics. And if it helps him to have Laurie there cheering him on, then why shouldn't she do it?"

"Well, Laurie, is that really what you want to do?" Mrs. Hudson asked, putting all sorts of doubts into her daughter's mind. A dismal way to begin a Monday morning.

"Look, Mom, I think I can manage my own life, thank you," she said frostily, pulling down the pretty rose-and-white cap her mother had crocheted for her the previous year. She tied the long matching scarf around her neck with an emphatic jerk, and yet when she turned to the mirror for one last look, it was clear that this conversation had given her a grim expression. She forced a smile, pecked her mother on the cheek, hugged her father, who returned to his newspaper a second later, and left for school.

Bob was standing in front of the main door of Edgewood High, chatting with Mike and Jim, members of the Gang, but when he saw Laurie he walked over to her. He was smiling, as if he were as glad to see Laurie as she was to see him, and when he kissed her, neither more nor less passionately than any other time, she was reassured. They were together again after an endless weekend.

The bell rang, and they had to separate for classes but promised to meet later.

A few comments pleased Laurie, although it was difficult to believe she had been Homecoming Queen. In a way it was last week's news.

"Hey, Laurie, you looked super Friday night."

"Your pictures in the paper were gorgeous. Will you autograph one for me?"

"My kid sister wants to be just like you when she grows up."

Laurie laughed as graciously as she could. "She'll probably change her mind!"

She thanked her friends for the compliments, yet she felt as though she were acting. The little puppet, Laurie, who smiled and acted sweetly toward everyone, hid a darker Laurie who felt threatened by a shadow so tiny she could hardly define it. Yet it was there. *"I have a little shadow that goes in and out with me, and what can be the use of him is more than I can see."* So went the Robert Louis Stevenson poem she had learned as a child. It was easy to understand physical shadows, but this one that could not be seen became menacing.

Was it possible she was psychic, foretelling a disaster?

But what could it be? It made no sense.

Sally Winchester, one of the girls in the Gang, a slender, elegant blond, stopped Laurie in the hall before math class to tell her with unexpected praise that she had acted handsomely all weekend.

"You took everything in stride. Not too nervous, not brash. You know, Laurie, you have poise!" Sally had nodded her head to emphasize her sincerity. Yet again that tiny doubt bothered Laurie, who no longer felt sure of herself — if she ever had.

For the first time, math class become comforting. She plunged herself into a thicket of algebra problems, finding them easier than human equations. In math, a problem works out or it doesn't, and shadows do not lurk among the figures.

At one point, however, she wondered if perhaps it was only natural for her to feel less than enthusiastic this dismal Monday morning. "After-pains," her mother would have called it. "After something big in your life like having a baby, or winning a prize, or performing in a play, whatever, it's natural to feel let down afterward. But it's not fatal. Eventually you go on to other things."

Of course, Laurie said to herself, and relieved that nothing was really wrong, concentrated fiercely on the problems before her and scored a ninety on a quiz.

Bob was already sitting in his seat in American history class, which he and Laurie took together. He was trying to catch up on the homework he hadn't done over the weekend. He was bright enough to pull off a passing grade when necessary and really could easily have topped the class. But Bob didn't really care.

"Hi, darling," Laurie whispered as she slipped into her seat on his left. He always kept the seat on his right side empty and put his jacket there. Laurie was comforted once more as she felt his warmth beside her. Right away Bob asked about the homework assignment. "Do we have to know all the stuff in chapter ten?" Laurie started to explain the work to him, until his concentration dissolved and his eyes, like those of practically everyone else in the class, focused on a new girl who had just walked up to the teacher. This was the girl who had smiled so winningly at Bob from the principal's office Friday afternoon. She attracted attention like a magnet. *She's really beautiful when she smiles,* Laurie thought, with her thick auburn hair and green eyes, which were set off by a soft lavender sweater and a violet corduroy skirt.

Mr. Boynton, the bored, bald history teacher, read the slip of paper the new girl had given him, then coughed for attention. "We have a new member in our class. This is Alison Wood. Where are you from, Alison?"

"L.A.," she said with barely contained laughter in her voice.

"Well, let's welcome Alison with the graciousness for which Edgewood High is so well known."

He spoke ironically, of course, but actually the class gave her a flattering greeting with whistles and cheers from the boys and a cordial acknowledgment from the girls. Then she did laugh and this time she lifted her hand and wiggled her fingers to accept the welcome. Mr. Boynton looked around for an empty seat and found the one beside Bob, so she walked over and slipped into it as he removed his jacket.

There was that smile again! She gave Laurie a quick, flashy hello but returned to the more serious business of grinning at Bob. She had a flirtatious way of opening her eyes wide and then letting her lids drop, only to open them suddenly again.

Laurie realized that here was the shadow she had feared. The depression following Homecoming had nothing to do with it. Alison from L.A. was bad, bad news, and Laurie hardly knew what to do about it.

Bob, falling over himself to be helpful, was already showing Alison how far they had advanced in American history. Laurie heard him repeating the information she had just given him, and he hinted that if Alison wanted to catch up with the class, he would share his notes with her. Laurie suppressed a frantic desire to jab her elbow into Bob's ribs, but Alison beamed as she thanked Bob for being so helpful. And then class began. Laurie did not hear a word of it.

When it was over, Bob turned to her. "Hi, honey, remember you said you'd come over to the pool today and time me? I'm sure lookin' forward to it."

His voice took on the silken tones he used when he wanted a favor from someone. Laurie was tempted to tell him what he could do with the pool — go jump in it — but if she refused to help him, then surely he would ask Alison. And Alison would say all right in tones as sugary as Bob's. It would never do.

"Bob, darlin'," Laurie said, imitating Bob's wheedling Southern tones. "Ah'll be there. You can't keep me away."

He missed the sarcasm.

"Terrific. I can always count on you, Laurie."

All day she tried to calm her rising fears. Maybe she was making too much of this smile-machine called Alison. Sooner or later someone would have to let her know that Bob and Laurie were a couple, and Alison would back off. Wishful thinking? But it was possible that Bob, who believed in winning people over, was simply practicing his skills on the new girl. He always had been faithful to Laurie, no doubt of that. If it were necessary he would tell Alison about Laurie.

Seeking reassurances, Laurie found one more. The final consolation was that Alison was probably one of those girls who flirted with everyone. By the end of the day she would have found at least five other blond giants nearly as handsome as Bob.

So forget it, Laurie. You don't have to worry.

Laurie worked harder in gym that day than she ever had before. Although she enjoyed watching athletic events, she thought of herself as nonathletic. Yet an hour of intensive gymnastics made her feel much better about everything.

Bob was already swimming in the outdoor pool when Laurie arrived later that afternoon. She shivered as she sat on the bench and wondered how the three boys in the pool could slash through the water so intently. She admired them greatly. Bob moved swiftly and rhythmically like some sea creature, faster and more graceful than the other two swimmers. *He's really great*, she thought, as his powerful, tanned body cut through the water rhythmically at a tremendous speed.

He looked up, caught sight of Laurie, and neatly hoisted himself out of the pool. He wrapped a huge white towel around his shoulders, white against his tan, his hair blond even when wet and plastered against his head.

"Bob, you're fantastic, and training hasn't even begun."

"It has for the others, and I'll have to catch up for the February meet. I've got a long way to go. Laurie, here's the stopwatch. Will you time me now and then later, so that I can tell what's happening?"

"Sure."

He bent down to give her a wet kiss. Then as she yelled "Start," while standing at the end of the pool, he dived in and began to swim. Laurie watched him and timed him, but she was getting chilled. The skies above took on a November mournfulness, streaks of depressing, cold blue mingled with sullen clouds. A loud cawing above caught her attention as three black crows came flying over the pool, dipping slightly as though to land. Then, rising high again, they shrieked at her and disappeared into the gray skies. Was this a symbol, a warning of bad luck?

Don't be so silly, Laurie told herself; they're only birds. Sometimes Laurie spoke to herself as though some big sister lived within her, a sensible sister who scolded her, yet reassured her when she feared unknown things. The birds had seemed ominous.

"Okay, what was it that time?" Bob asked, coming to the edge of the pool.

"Bob, I'm sorry. I lost count. I was watching the crows. Please do it again, and I promise —"

"Okay. Laurie, you're getting absentminded lately. Haven't you noticed?"

"No. I can't remember it happening before. Anyway, I was only watching the birds, and they're gone. Try it again, will you?"

This time as Bob sped back and forth across the pool, leaving a wake of excited foam behind him, she watched the time carefully. Was she really absentminded? The thought made her uncomfortable.

"There, Bob, that's great. Much better," she said enthusiastically.

"But it's not good enough," he said, his teeth clenched in the determination he so often showed when working out. Laurie could not imagine him swimming lazily for fun or rallying on the tennis court without keeping score. He had to win every time, every place, no matter what he was doing.

"Ten minutes more, Laurie, would you mind? And then we can go for a hot chocolate. I could use some sugar at this point."

"I could use some sweetness, too," Laurie said softly as she pulled her jacket around her more tightly. The day may have been all right for swimming, but standing still and observing was something else again. Ten minutes later he grabbed his towel, kissed her with a cold, wet thanks, and told her to wait in the Fiat for him.

The Dinky, that dear little red sports car, invariably made her feel better, as if she were someone else entirely, like a model in a magazine ad. Soon Bob was driving her to Angelo's, spoiling whatever appetites they may have had for dinner on hot chocolate and English muffins with jam. *See*, Laurie told herself, *everything is the way it used to be. It's all right.*

"You'll have to see the boat I think my father's going to buy. What a beauty! I've got a whole new fantasy, sailing around the world in it. Kind of scary but exciting."

"Yeah, exciting. And how would you go, east to west? Have you mapped it out yet?" Laurie was half-laughing, always delighted with Bob's dreams. He had already talked of getting himself a Cessna; he would go to Africa on safari; he would raise fighting dogs trained to kill and in that way he would make a killing — a profit; he would go into business with his father and set up a small real estate empire spreading over the county. Oddly enough, Laurie always found a thread of possibility in his fantasies. Suddenly he stopped.

"Laurie, you're one great listener. I go on and on, but you never talk about your fantasies. You must have some."

"Sure, but it's hard to talk about them."

"Come on now."

This was a new tack. Could Bob really care about her dreams? Up to this point they were limited but more or less clear, she thought: our wedding day; a small cottage to begin with, then with the coming of a family (one boy, one girl) a new house something like those on Strawberry Hill; a garden and a swimming pool and a car of my own — so many things. We would take trips all over the world, but my heart would always be with Bob, wherever we were.

"Mostly I have fantasies about you and me,"

Laurie said, and then put her fingers to her lips to cover a sudden embarrassment.

"Is that right?" Bob asked with a coldness that surprised Laurie. He changed the subject abruptly. "Want to go to the Varsity on Saturday? There's a great space-western coming."

"Sounds good," Laurie said.

He left some change and the two of them walked out to the Dinky. He stopped in front of her house and brushed her cheek with his lips, more dutifully than romantically.

"*Ciao*," Laurie said with false gaiety as she got out, but her smile faded as she walked up to the front door. A minor chord within her boded that things were not right after all.

F^{ive}

"Hey, Laurie, wait for me! I'm going to gym, too."

Three days had passed since Alison first came to Edgewood High. She rushed along the corridor to catch up with a reluctant Laurie. "Hi. I've been wanting to talk to you, but I haven't had a chance. You seem so friendly, I want to get to know you better."

"Do you really?" Laurie asked coldly, for it must have been obvious to Alison that her attitude was hardly friendly. But possibly Laurie had misjudged this new girl, who appeared to be genuinely warm. Perhaps she was not really flirting with Bob, only showing how enthusiastic she was. *Oh, yeah?* Laurie's other self, the wise older sister, remarked.

"Everyone's been telling me about how you were Homecoming Queen and everything. I wish I could have seen you. You must have been so proud!"

"It has to happen to someone."

"But not to just anyone. You have to be real special."

Laurie thought it was time to change the subject. "Do you think you'll like it here, Alison?"

"Really. It's neat. Not like L.A., believe me. I just wish I could get to know some people. It's kind of cliquey, isn't it?"

"In a way. Most high schools are. But there are lots of nice people here."

Alison put her hand on Laurie's as they were about to enter the dressing room. "Please, Laurie, would you tell me who's who and all that? I want to meet the right crowd, and you're the only one I could possibly ask." Her smile was one that said, "I love you, the world is beautiful, and won't you love me, too, because I love to be loved."

But Laurie winced at the tactic. She recognized the falseness of Alison's sweet smile because she had witnessed it before at the Hamiltons'. But *they* had been more subtle. She had been eleven when Bob gave her the first lesson in sweet talk. She had expressed some idea honestly but bluntly, and Bob had shaken his head.

"You're gonna make so many enemies, Laurie, by sayin' just what you mean straight out like that. Lookin' at a person can be the most important thing in the world, the difference between getting what you want and not getting it. That's what my father says. Look at someone as if he's the most special guy in the world and as if you don't want anything except for him to know how much you like him. Then you've got him in the palm of your hand."

"But Bob, isn't that lying?"

"A little white lie, that's all. It means you're making someone else feel happier and better. Honesty is overrated. Come on, practice on me. A wide smile, that's it. A soft voice — yeah, you got it!"

So she had tried it tentatively at first to see if it worked on other people, and it did. However, she still preferred to be direct when possible. Now this lesson that Bob taught her so long ago stood her in good stead, for she recognized at once that Alison wanted to use her.

"Hey, Alison, I don't want to be late for gym. Come on."

As they changed hurriedly into shorts and jerseys, they grinned at each other, but when Laurie caught sight of herself in the mirror, her teeth seemed bared like an animal about to snarl. Being hypocritical simply did not become her.

But the contest between Laurie and Alison was already on, an unnamed competition. Laurie had never dealt with it before, and the smile left her face as she entered the gym wondering how she would deal with the struggle she saw ahead of her.

After gym, Laurie walked to English class and sat down, baffled and upset. She was quite certain now that Alison was interested in Bob, and she didn't know what to do about it. *I'm not competitive*, she thought, *that's what's wrong.* Unlike Bob, who loved to fight fiercely and savagely, contrasting with the slow, sweet manner of talking that made him popular, Laurie was more direct in her speech and gentle in her actions. It was not in her nature to fight, and she had never had to fight for anything.

Of course, Bob will tell Alison off sooner or later, she tried to comfort herself. Once or twice other girls had tried to win him over, and he had gently but firmly let them know that he was going with Laurie — she was the one who wore his gold football.

In the row behind her, a few seats to the right, sat Gregory Munson. Every now and then, like today, she had the prickly sensation that he was watching her, but he'd never spoken to her at all. Possibly he associated her with the Gang, which was reputedly snobbish. He must know that she went with Bob, who was clearly responsible for not inviting him to that party so long ago. More than once Laurie had wanted to explain or to apologize, and yet his apparent aloofness stopped her each time. All she knew about him was that he was continually winning awards in track and that he spoke brilliantly in English class.

On that particular day she did not hear a word that Miss Karlson was saying about the American novel. Laurie could envision a smiling Alison whispering to Bob. Laurie sat upright in total lack of comprehension when Miss Karlson sternly directed a question at her.

"Laurie Hudson, what would you say characterized the American novel during the nineteenth century? What influences were most evident? Where would you find them?"

Laurie turned red, catching only the last few words of the question. Knowing that oral recitations counted for half the grade and she had not done very well so far this year, she hesitated, stammered, and was about to ask her to repeat the question when suddenly Greg Munson's voice, low and clear, began to answer it.

"Any number of influences can be noted. In the first place . . ."

If Miss Karlson had thought about interrupting him and letting him know it was not his question, she hesitated, for he spoke with such clarity and authority that he could only delight her. In fact, her beady expression softened.

"Well, Greg, obviously the question wasn't yours, but you answered it so capably, you've earned yourself an *A*. I hope the rest of you were taking notes. Now then, Laurie, a question for you — and try to keep awake this time."

The question this time was mercifully easy, and Laurie answered correctly, although without any of Greg's distinction.

When the class was finished, she was careful to approach Greg as they left the room.

"Thanks, Greg. You saved me from drowning in there."

"I don't know what you're talking about." His voice took on a certain frostiness. He must have known the question had clearly been directed at her.

"I was in a funk and didn't know what was going on at all. You answered the question that was meant for me. You were terrific, and it gave me the chance to wake up. I appreciate it, and I want you to know."

"If it helped you, fine, but this is the first I know about it. Your question and all that," he said, but his gray eyes twinkled. It was clear he knew very well he had saved her, but he was not about to become friendly.

"See you around," he said, and vanished among the crowd in the hall.

Mercifully, this unexpected event surprised her, so that for a while she was able to forget about Alison and Bob as well. She wondered about Greg, found him somewhat mysterious, even fascinating. She also wondered if he had a girl friend.

What if Alison were to go after him and

leave Bob alone? The possibility no sooner occurred to her than she found herself nearly crying no, out loud. Even though Greg made no advances to her, not even those of friendship, the thought that he might like Alison infuriated her.

Really, she said to herself at last, *there's no need to become so upset. After all, it's Bob that you care about, isn't it? Of course, silly, of course.*

Six

On Friday night, eight of the Gang, including Bob and Laurie, went bowling in Edgewood. Afterward, they drove fifteen miles or so to a pizzeria, even though Edgewood had several good pizza parlors. Laurie supposed it was a way of showing off, but it was so good to be with Bob again and the others in the Gang — without Alison in sight — that she felt reassured and became more lively than ever.

Much later as Bob took her home, she asked, "Is it still on for tomorrow?"

"Is what still on?"

"You know, the movie. *Space Drifters*. Remember on Monday afternoon you asked me to go?"

"Laurie, you must be dreaming. I don't remember that at all."

"But we talked about it. You wanted me to go."

"I don't like to say this again, Laurie, but you really have been awfully absentminded lately."

Laurie knew very well that he had asked her, yet now he was making her doubt herself. Was it possible he was trying to provoke a fight?

"Are you sure you don't remember, Bob? It doesn't really matter, does it? If you want to see it, I'd still like to go." She spoke softly, and it was clear she would not argue about it.

But he frowned. "I don't remember it, Laurie, and I'm sorry there's a misunderstanding. My parents are having a thing, and I have to stay around. You know how it is."

Laurie knew how it was — an excuse. Bob looked her directly in the eye, and she remembered once he had told her that the most convincing way to lie was to engage the eyes of the other person.

"Sure, I guess that's how it is then," Laurie said lightly, for it would never do to make an issue of it. Then she put her face up close to his, as if asking for a kiss, a flirtatious kind of playfulness. Bob grinned, relieved that the matter was settled, and then he kissed her so hard and held her so close that she felt he would crush her. Then he released her. But he said nothing. Nothing at all.

"It was nice going out tonight. Thanks, Bob."

"I could have had a better score in bowling, but I guess it was fun, wasn't it? Good night, Laurie, have a nice weekend."

He did not even wait until she reached the front door before roaring away into the night. It was barely ten o'clock, which would give him time for another date with someone else if he wanted it.

Laurie spent the weekend alone. Nobody called. Nobody from the Gang. Not even Linda Cahill phoned to say hello, as she sometimes did. On Saturday, Laurie cleaned house for her mother as a way of earning money for the Homecoming dress, and took a long, solitary walk with her dog, Patch; on Sunday afternoon, she treated Tracy to the movies.

On Monday, Alison bounced up to Laurie in the locker room of the gym as though they were the best of friends. That morning in American history she had thrown Laurie a deceptively sweet smile and spent the rest of the period playing a game that Laurie grimly entitled "Catching Bob." *How does she do it?* Laurie wondered. She could move her eyes in a certain way, let them crinkle at the edges as if she were laughing, or make them wide and dreamy as if she were falling in love. *Is she really charming?* Laurie asked herself, and decided that she was. It was also clear she couldn't be trusted.

"Laurie, have lunch with me. Say yes. Please. I'll treat."

"Thanks, but I brought my own lunch. The caf food is too starchy."

"Oooh, no wonder you have such a nice figure. But please sit with me. You can have your own lunch. I get so lonesome here. It's hard to be new."

"I'll bet," Laurie said. Was it possible she was becoming catty? There was always the chance that Alison did like her and wanted her friendship. And it was also possible that Bob was simply being nice to a new girl who had not yet found friends.

Really? asked the invisible big sister in Laurie's mind. *Isn't it also possible that your enemy is playing a fascinating game? Watch out!*

"Let's sit in the corner because I want our talk to be very private. Confidential!" Alison whispered. She bought herself lunch, a huge green salad which made Laurie's tiny tub of cottage cheese and carrot sticks look miserable in comparison.

"It's like this, Laurie. Some boys have asked me out, and I want to know about them. Peter Gorham, Mike Chatfield, Robbie Myer. Do you know them? Do you know someone named Rickie Morehouse? He's a doll."

"You've been really busy, haven't you? Leave Rick alone, Alison. He's going with Charlene, who's a very nice girl, and if you break them up it won't really do you any good." Laurie had to check her voice for it was beginning to sound severe. "Mike Chatfield? He's okay, sort of nice. Robbie Myer is great and very good-looking. Don't you think so?"

Laurie had recommended Robbie because he was not a member of the Gang, and she thought he was very charming, a nice fly to get caught in Alison's web. *Oh, no,* Laurie thought, *catty again!*

Alison smiled at all of this, the friendly, toothy, hey-I-really-like-you smile. Laurie was tempted to say, "Don't waste it on me," but held her tongue.

"Robbie's nice. The boys here are really attentive, not spoiled the way they are in L.A. The one I really wonder about is Bob. You know, Bob? He's the one that sits between us in American history. He's so helpful."

Laurie became so angry that she held her breath, but Alison only blinked her eyes innocently. "Don't you like Bob?"

Of course Alison knew, she had to know, that Bob was the Homecoming King and that the two of them had been cast as the Lovers all through high school — even before. It had always been that way. Besides, Laurie had seen Alison talking with Sally and Teri and some other girls in the Gang, and surely they would have told her. Alison was out to make trouble, but Laurie would not be had, not for a minute. She got up abruptly.

"Alison, I have to finish a paper for English, so if you'll excuse me . . ."

"But you haven't finished your lunch. You're not leaving all those molasses cookies? They look homemade. Did you make them?"

"If you want to finish my lunch, go right ahead," Laurie said with such scorn, it surprised her that Alison did not throw the cookies in her face. Beyond such mistakes, Alison smiled with insincerity, and not to be outdone, Laurie grinned stiffly back at her. A truce that fooled nobody.

Yet as Laurie left the lunchroom the smile vanished. She held the tiny gold football, hoping it would reassure her. If only she had someone to talk with, but nobody offered her open arms, a shoulder to lean on, and a willing ear. Bob would be the last person she could confide in — how very strange! But now that she needed a true friend, she realized none of the girls in the Gang would do. Though her mother would make more sense than anyone, she could hardly confide her fears.

She would have to be her own best friend. Of course, her imaginary big sister was not lacking in advice. *You must think positively. Keep your faith in Bob. Imagine victory, not failure.*

Laurie conjured up a short drama. Alison was putting her hand on his arm and practically asking for a kiss. "Listen, Alison, honey," Bob would say, "you better try this with someone else because Laurie and I go together. That's how it is. She's my girl, and there's nobody else.

Look at Mark over there. I think he would like you very much. Go ahead, Alison." And then Bob would take Laurie in his arms. "I'm glad she's out of the way," he would say.

But how could Laurie bring about this satisfying scene? It wasn't as if she could write it down, give out the parts, and say this is the way it should be.

Still, she had the best opportunities. Christmas vacation would be coming up soon. As usual she'd go to the big dance with Bob, and then the Hamiltons would most likely invite her up to Squaw Valley to their cabin. This year she would ski better than ever, would exercise long before they tried the slopes. Bob would be proud of her then. They'd play in the snow, tumbling and rolling around like bear cubs. On the long, wintry evenings they would sit before the fire; she would kiss him and he would hold her tight. She would get him to talk about love.

These fantasies became pictures inside her head, and she held to them as if they were the magic that would keep away the fear that was building in her. She had no sooner settled in her seat in English class than another picture blotted out the others, one that came against her will: Bob was skiing down a slope with Alison, the snow gently spraying out behind them. At one point he turned to look at her.

"Oh, no!" Laurie cried softly, but loud enough so that the people around her heard. Then, even more upsetting, her books fell to the floor. "Darn," she said as she bent to pick them up, only to bump heads with Greg Munson, who was gathering the math papers that had fluttered out of her book.

"Are you okay?" he asked in a voice that was audible only to Laurie.

"Of course. I just remembered that I forgot my essay at home, and I stayed up to midnight to do it, too. I feel so silly." She giggled out of embarrassment, but Greg did not appear to be taken in.

"You're sure everything is all right?" he asked, as though he were concerned.

"All right, Laurie, if you forgot your paper it's hardly a tragedy. It's not really due until tomorrow anyway, so let's get to work, everyone," Miss Karlson said vigorously. "You're sure you're all right, Laurie?"

"I'm fine," Laurie said, already aware of the two spots that always appeared on her cheeks when she felt cornered. If she were Pinocchio, she figured, her nose would be a yard long at this point and still growing.

But something was to be said for the school routine and soon she felt calmer. She found it quite possible to meet with the other cheerleaders after school, for one more important game was coming up and they wanted to try a new routine. She shouted until her voice became hoarse, she jumped in the air, kicked, kneeled, and literally danced through the new cheers. Bob would see that she was good, really good, even if only one more game was left. The concentration brought relief from her thoughts of Alison, but as soon as the practice was over she felt haunted once more. She trudged home and threw herself onto the bed.

What will happen next? she asked herself. *Oh God, what will happen next?*

Seven

"Laurie, something's bothering you. Come on and let it out. You can confide in your dear old mom." Mrs. Hudson spoke lightly, but her voice showed concern. She had made hot biscuits that morning, hoping to coax Laurie's failing appetite.

"Thanks, dear old Mom," Laurie answered as playfully as she could, "but there's nothing to confide. Everything's peachy."

"Are you sure? Doesn't seem that way. Maybe I can help — you know I can keep a secret."

Although Laurie and her mother were alone in the kitchen and spoke quietly, Mr. Hudson had overheard as he walked through the door.

"What she needs is a good breakfast, a good

lunch, and a good dinner," he said in his hearty voice. "That's all that's wrong. She wants to be built up."

Laurie groaned softly as she protested. "Dad, I eat far too much. See, I'm getting fat..."

She tried to pinch the flesh around her waist to show him, but there was nothing to pinch. Still, the thought of eating anything upset her, even though her mother's light, steaming biscuits were more tempting than the most lavish ad in a magazine.

"It's *late!*" Laurie cried, running to her bedroom as the tears spilled over. Her parents looked at each other helplessly, and she heard Tracy ask loudly, "Is she cryin' because Bob doesn't come over anymore?"

Shut up! Laurie refrained from shouting it but was shocked that she even thought at all about talking that way to anyone.

If Bob had told her outright that everything was off, one clean break, Laurie knew it would have hurt more at the time yet in the long run would be the kindest thing to do. She would have said to her family, "Bob and I are no longer going together, and I don't want to talk about it."

But in the weeks that had passed since Alison's arrival, he had complicated the issue by saying nothing. He invited Laurie out to a movie or to a coffee house after she had watched him at football practice, and he still seemed to need her there. He told her she was his good luck symbol and it meant more to him than anything else in the world for her to be there. Yet Bob now walked around openly with Alison in the lunchroom and outside the school in the morning. Once Laurie saw him driving with Alison in the Dinky when he didn't have after-school practice. And he had yet to ask her to the Christmas Dance.

Still, Laurie had excuses for everything. Maybe he took it for granted that they would go to that big affair together — it had always been that way. Maybe Alison came on so strong he didn't know how to put her down. Or, perhaps he was infatuated with Alison now but would come back to Laurie, and their love would be all the stronger for having survived.

One moment she was filled with hope and trust, and the next she feared she would never see Bob again. One morning as she sat in desperate loneliness in American history, he turned to her unexpectedly and asked her to go to a party at Punky Scott's that night. She had agreed almost too eagerly although Punky drank too much and his parties invariably became brutish. As she expected, Bob drank a lot of hard liquor and slipped into a sullen silence. He'd driven Laurie home and parked in front of her house. Laurie had thought he might talk seriously with her, but he'd been too drunk and there had been no getting to him. With lackluster eyes and slack jaw he mumbled, "G'night," and drove off unsteadily.

Laurie feared for him. How could he keep

up with his training if he drank so much! And wasn't it possible that he drank more than usual because he may have been caught between Alison and herself?

Then this would be her challenge. Laurie's eyes flashed as she determined not to give up Bob without fighting for him. It did not occur to her until much later how odd an attitude this was, as though Bob were a possession, something she *owned*. Nevertheless, that's what she thought at that particular time.

For one thing, you have to wear more interesting clothes, Laurie's imaginary big sister said. Laurie hesitated, for she still had to earn money to pay for her Homecoming dress. But desperate situations call for daring measures, so one day after school she walked in and out of Edgewood's five boutiques in search of the magic garment that would send Bob running back to her. At last she found it, a pale pink fluff of a sweater, adorably feminine with a lavender ribbon strung through the crocheted trim.

"May I try it on?" she asked the salesgirl. Laurie's image of herself was as a healthy all-American girl whose boyfriend took the spotlight in the sports arena. She wore classic clothes for the most part. The Homecoming dress had been a departure from that image, and now standing before the mirror, Laurie became enchanted with this new aspect of herself — a softer, more feminine girl. The mohair caressed her and the silly, charming ribbon drawn through the openwork added a deliciously frivolous touch. Laurie bought it even though it would take several months to pay for it.

"Oh, Laurie," her mother said later when she saw it. "It's charming, but why didn't you let me know you wanted something like this? I could whip up a sweater exactly like this in two or three evenings for a fraction of what you're paying for this. Perhaps you can bring it back."

"Perhaps I can, but I won't," Laurie said. She wanted that sweater for the very next morning. Time was slipping by all too quickly.

"I hope you'll have the good sense not to wear it to school," Mrs. Hudson said, but when she saw the set of Laurie's lips and knew that's exactly what she planned to do, she sighed and gave up. "I guess when I was sixteen, I would have felt like that, too. It's a shame you'll be having to pay for it for such a long time."

"Oooh, why are you always so sensible?" Laurie asked sharply and then mumbled, "I didn't mean it that way. I have to have the sweater, that's all. Don't worry. I'll pay for it."

And that was it. This was war and now she had to act decisively. The sweater took on magic qualities; it would bring Bob back when he saw her in a new way.

Several girls admired it the next morning, and Laurie's heart beat swiftly as she slipped into her seat in American history a minute after Bob arrived. Unfortunately Alison bounced in at the same time, and Bob was immediately caught up in some foolish anecdote she was relating with exaggerated facial expressions that seemed to amuse him.

When she finished, Bob turned to Laurie. "You're here? I didn't even see you come in."

Laurie paid no attention to the lie, but sat up straight and touched the gold football that lay quietly over the sweater. She smiled serenely, coquettishly, but without giggling. She wanted to present a femininity that would contrast with Alison's overacting. Bob said, "H'm," as he judged the sweater, and he must have been aware of the Chloé Laurie had just sprayed on — it was his favorite scent.

"Hey, that's some sweater, Laurie. I've never seen you in anything like it."

"Thanks, Bob. I'm glad you like it."

"It's soft. What is this anyway, mohair? A change for you, isn't it? I always liked the classic sweaters you wear, the dark green one, that red sleeveless vest or whatever it is. This is really different."

"I'm glad you noticed," Laurie said. He appeared to be thinking of something more that he had to say, and at last came out with it bluntly.

"It's not you, Laurie, it just isn't you, all that soft, kitteny stuff. Now Alison could wear it; wow, she'd be fantastic in that color! I really like you better in that alpine green pullover and that sporty navy blue sweater with the cable stitch. Honey, this isn't *you*."

"All right, all right, let's get started!" Mr. Boynton shouted over the buzz of conversation. Bob turned to his notebook while Laurie sat crestfallen. Alison was waving her hand with an answer to a question Mr. Boynton had asked. Then she stood up to deliver a long-winded, though inaccurate answer. Not a single boy in the class, including Bob, could take their eyes away from her.

Laurie sat alone, facing the bitterness of defeat. Without doing anything at all, Alison had won this battle. It would cost Laurie dearly for a long, long time.

E^{ight}

The weekend yawned emptily for Laurie, not a date, not a baby-sitting engagement. Nothing. If only someone would call, anyone at all. . . . But why would any boy call when it had always been understood that Laurie and Bob went together? Nobody would stand between them.

"Where's Bob these days?" Mr. Hudson asked tactlessly on Friday night.

"His family went up to the cabin," Laurie explained. In the past she would have been invited to join them. Now she wondered if Alison was taking her place.

Whispers and rumors were probably circulating around school and among the Gang about the possible breakup of the Lovers. Yet nothing was settled, and the very uncertainty of it plunged Laurie into such desperation she was ready to call it all off.

Yet how could she do so when she loved Bob, when she had always loved him?

She decided to wait it out. If he asked her to the Christmas Dance, then she would know they had come through the Alison scare safely. And if he didn't . . . but, oh, he would, *he would*, she prayed. It was only the waiting that was so difficult.

On Friday night, the distinguished chorus of Edgewood High gave its Christmas concert, and Laurie went alone. She had sometimes heard the chorus rehearse and knew then that its splendid reputation was well deserved. Bob had never wanted to attend any of their concerts since he didn't care for *that* kind of music. "If I wanted to sleep, I'd go," he had said, and Laurie had acquiesced.

She wore dark clothes, sat in the back, and hoped that nobody would recognize her. The auditorium filled rapidly, not only with the parents of the singers but with faculty, townspeople, and — surprisingly enough — many students. Laurie had taken for granted that crowds would overflow at football and basketball games, but at a concert where music wasn't rock or country and western, she hadn't expected such a turnout.

"Aw, singing, playing in the orchestra, all that kinda stuff is fun for the people who are doing it, but nobody really wants to listen to it," Bob had once said. Laurie had not agreed, but had kept her opinions to herself.

"Even so I'd love to try out for it."

"Sure, but Laurie, you know I need you. Anyway, you're a terrific cheerleader; you wouldn't want to give that up, would you? Do you know how much the team relies on the cheerleaders?"

She had given in. Laurie had liked cheerleading, but now as she sat waiting for the concert to begin, she was angry at herself for having wasted so much time sitting in the bleachers, sweating through Indian-summer heat, or shivering through the foggy cold to cheer Bob during *his* practice. Possibly she could have made the chorus. But she loved Bob and had wanted to help him.

In any event, the time was past and couldn't be relived.

A hush fell over the house as the curtains parted and the chorus walked onstage, the girls in long gowns of a softly gleaming blue material and the boys in dark suits. Applause filled the hall when Mr. Rappaport, the tall, slender conductor, walked smoothly across the stage and bowed to the audience.

The program celebrated international music of the winter solstice. Laurie sat mesmerized as the chorus sang three early madrigals from France and England; two lively songs for Chanukah; a Japanese song about winter; three short, drum-accompanied carols from Africa; a transcribed Eskimo poem set to music; and two contemporary winter songs. The last third of the program was devoted to Christmas carols, some traditional and some new, all sung with such tenderness that tears came to Laurie's eyes. Now she felt herself relaxing, as if all the fears in her life were becoming less important as she became lost in the intricate weavings and changing harmonies of the familiar melodies.

If only I could have been up there, Laurie mused as she walked out of the auditorium after the concert.

She caught a brief glimpse of someone familiar in the crowd — Greg Munson! How nice it would be if she could talk with him about the concert! He would understand how she felt about the music, she was certain of that. But then he had hardly said hello to her at any time. And was it possible that he was walking with a tall, good-looking girl whom Laurie had never seen before? So that's how it was!

Even so, the spell of the music lasted. It had come to her like a gift, and she walked home serenely in the cold, starry night.

On Saturday morning another surprise came for Laurie — a telephone call from Linda Cahill, who invited Laurie over to lunch. "I haven't seen you for a long time, Laurie. There'll just be the two of us. And I'll make fantastic spaghetti. So how about it?"

Linda, a strong, independent girl who lived

with her divorced mother in a small home like the Hudsons, had a circle of friends quite unlike the Gang. Yet now and then she and Laurie managed to get together, and at those times Laurie wondered why they couldn't have been better friends. But she knew the answer — she'd given all her time to Bob.

Now Laurie toyed with the spaghetti, wishing she could enjoy it. Linda cooked well, did everything well.

"This is a wonderful sauce. How do you make it anyway? Oh, Linda, you were so nice to call me."

"Not at all. I wanted to see you. Anyway, something's not right. Want to talk about it?"

"I can't. It's shameful. Oh, Linda, everything is awful!" Laurie hadn't meant to talk about her troubles, much less to cry. She dabbed at her eyes.

"It's about Bob, isn't it?"

"Of course. I don't understand it. We've gone together since we were ten. There's never been anyone else. Little kids can fall in love just like older people; they say it's puppy love and laugh at it, but it's real just the same. Bob and I have always been together. And now . . . I guess you know. He's going with Alison. But he goes with me, too, so I can't tell."

"Shall I be blunt? It will hurt, but the truth may set you free, as they say."

"I'm so hurt now, it couldn't be worse. *Not* knowing is the hardest thing of all."

"All right, Laurie. Bob is crazy about Alison, taking her everywhere. I worked with Louise Scott on a science project, and she told me. When Bob tells you he's working with his father, chances are he's out with Alison. But you knew that, didn't you?"

"I didn't know. I guessed."

"Don't give up. Alison is a strange girl — in some ways she's a nasty little mink — but when she's not trying to get every guy within sight, she can be very nice. Oddly enough, she reminds me of you — she's very enthusiastic, like you. But you are really nice, and she isn't. I hope Bob comes to his senses. I mean it. On the other hand, if he doesn't come back, console yourself. It's better to find out that he's ready to take out other girls now than to wait until after you're married."

"Linda, I love him. I always have. It's real."

"But you can't expect life to work out so smoothly."

"Careful. You're beginning to sound like my mother."

Linda laughed. "Well, your mom is one neat lady. And maybe she's right. Mine always thinks she's right. About *everything*. Now tell me, has Bob asked you to the Christmas Dance?"

"Not yet."

"Hmm. Maybe he will and maybe he won't, is that it? Alison is doing everything she can to interest Bob, and she's doing pretty well. But it's not certain for her either. So don't give up."

"What am I supposed to do?"

"Fight fire with fire."

"Ho, ho, ho. How do I do that?"

"Eat your spaghetti, and let me think for a minute."

Laurie pushed it around with her fork, seeing no solution whatever. Then Linda brightened.

"Okay, I've got it. You give a party for the Gang."

"In our silly little house — when they live in those redwood palaces on Strawberry Hill? I wouldn't dare."

"Sure you would! Listen, the best parties are those where there's little space. Then people have to be sociable. See?"

"But our house is so . . . small and plain. The furniture's old and scratched. We don't have a good stereo. You should see where *they* live."

Linda waved her hand in the air as if to ward off any complaints. Her mother was a business executive, and Laurie imagined that Linda would also have an important career someday. She talked about the party.

"Listen! This is a special party, not like those you've gone to, but something different. Turn out all the lights and have candles, maybe one or two small lamps to keep people from falling over each other. That will hide the furniture and make the party mysterious. Then, it's Christmas, so we can pick up pine boughs, fir boughs, whatever — if we go out to the hills we can get them for free. How about that? And we'll have great food. I'll contribute two cheese-cakes. That's a promise. With raspberry topping."

"Linda, you're marvelous, but really, I can't —"

"Do you have a better idea? It will work. Bob will see you in a new way; it will still be you but a different side of you, the gracious hostess. You can wear pants, and I've got a slinky top my mother got on sale. It's too big but we can cut it down. You'll look glamorous."

"Linda, it's so complicated. For one thing, you know about my parents and alcohol. They won't let me have it."

"Well, what about cider? Hey — I know, you can make a hot, steaming cider with lots of cloves. It's like grog, but with cider instead of wine. We can get around that, don't worry."

"But you have to have music. Our stereo is awful, and we don't have the right kind of records."

"Simple. You ask everyone to bring his or her favorite tape. Bob has a tape deck, doesn't he? Ask him to bring it. Problem solved. *Also*, your mother has always wanted you to have a party. Didn't she once say she'd make all the lasagna you wanted if you'd have one? Maybe she's a little hurt that you don't use your own house."

"I know. Don't think it hasn't occurred to me. Okay, there's one more snag to this idea,

Linda. I'll ask the Gang, but what if Bob or someone brings Alison?"

"If she comes, she comes. It's a chance you'll have to take."

A sixth sense was telling Laurie to forget the party, but Linda sounded so certain that it would work. There seemed to be no other way out, so she held on to the idea.

"Laurie, listen to me. My theory is this: Bob is caught between the two of you. Everything is in the air. This may be the turning point."

"And if he chooses Alison?"

"It's best to know now. *But it hasn't happened yet.*"

"If Bob wanted to write a book called *How to Get Rid of a Girl Friend,* he could do it. Rule No. 1. Forget she's there and turn to the new girl who's cutting in. No. 2. When you talk with the girl friend you want to ditch, do it charitably as if she were really ugly and you are doing her a favor by saying a few kind words. No. 3. Whisper with the new girl friend, laugh at her jokes, but by no means explain anything to the old girl friend."

"Hey, Laurie. Are you sure you really love Bob? Or are you just angry?"

"I don't know anymore. I'm so mixed up, Linda. Of course I love Bob."

"Then fight for him, Laurie. Fight fire with fire. He'll respect you if nothing else."

"It's a gamble, isn't it?"

"Everything in life is a gamble. *Everything.*

If you lose, you lose. But if you don't try . . ."

"Right. Okay then. Linda, you're the first person I'm inviting."

"Thanks a lot, but Kenny and I wouldn't fit in. I'd love to help you put it on, if you want me to."

"I'd love it, if you feel like doing it. You're terrific. I'm feeling better already, as if I'm doing something instead of simply waiting. Of course I have to ask my mom, and I have to ask Bob and everyone."

"No matter what happens, you look ten times more alive now than when you came in. So, let's keep in touch."

"I wish I could stay and talk with you about it, Linda, but this morning a baby-sitting job came through and I need some cash so I'd better go. Thanks for everything. And we will keep in touch, okay?"

"Good luck, Laurie!"

"A party? Terrific." Her parents liked the idea. Mr. Hudson began to say something about its being better than moping but Mrs. Hudson, far more tactful, drowned him out by talking loudly about taking up the rug so everyone could dance. Laurie sighed at their backwardness when they wouldn't let her have a bar, but secretly she was relieved to resort to mulled cider.

The date Laurie chose was a Friday night, one week before the Christmas Dance. It might turn the tide or it might not, but it would be better than staying home and watching TV by herself.

"Hi, Bob," Laurie said at the beginning of American history class. She seldom saw him anymore, but she was careful to appear bright-eyed. "I have something to ask you."

"Oh, you want my autograph?" he joked, then became more serious. "How are you anyway? I never get to see you anymore. I miss you, Laurie."

"I miss you, too."

Did he mean it? Was he possibly sincere or was this only his sweetness-everywhere-to-everyone policy?

"Bob, how about having a party for the Gang over my house? I've been thinking about having it this coming Friday night."

"You mean it? Laurie, that would be fantastic. We were talking about getting together and it turns out that nobody can have a party this Friday. Mike's folks are having one, mine are giving an important dinner, Sally's parents are away, and Alan is being punished for taking his father's car without permission. Can you imagine? Anyway, it would be perfect."

"Do you think everyone would bring a favorite tape? And could you bring your tape deck? It would help out a lot."

"Right. Want me to bring some wine? Everyone'd be glad to bring along some ... ahem ... liquid refreshment."

"Thanks, but you know my folks. Listen, this is just for the Gang, nobody else."

"Sure. Want me to ask everyone?" He was already beginning to take over, and Laurie sensed danger there. The new idea burst in the nick of time. "Actually, I'd rather you didn't because I'd like to write out the invitations myself. Something Christmassy. It is special, you know."

"Sounds great, Laurie," he said, and she grinned. Alison would not receive an invitation and, if Laurie were lucky, would be too proud to crash.

"Laurie," Bob continued, "I have to go out to Starkie's Kennels after school, 'cause I'm getting myself a Doberman. He's still too young to leave his mom, but I'd like you to see him."

"I'd love to, Bob, but I promised Mrs. Burns I'd baby-sit, and she'll be waiting for me. Could we do it tomorrow?"

"Sorry, I've got a practice coming up. Maybe Alison will want to go. And speak of the devil, here she is!"

Alison slid into her seat just as class began. Immediately Bob turned to her as though Laurie didn't exist.

Nine

Aside from one or two pajama parties Laurie had had when she was nine or ten, she had never thrown a party.

"And now you're making up for it," Mrs. Hudson said. "But really, honey, you don't have to do a whole spring cleaning for it."

Nevertheless, Laurie insisted this party had to be perfect. She'd bought some invitations at the stationery store and mailed them out, which surprised and pleased the Gang since they had never been quite so formal about their parties.

Then Laurie began to clean the house, working at it every day after school. "Laurie, it's not necessary to scrub and wax the floors and wash the windows and take down the paintings," her mother said. Laurie wondered if her feelings were hurt, as though Laurie felt the house wasn't good enough. Unfortunately, that was exactly how Laurie felt, but she was careful to be as diplomatic as possible.

"Mom, we're making a piñata and filling it with favors and bags of candy, and when the kids whack at it blindfolded, they might break the glass on the paintings. You wouldn't want Aunt Lou's watercolor hurt."

When Laurie took down her father's treasure, a garish portrait of an Indian painted on black velvet that he'd won at the county fair when he was a boy, she explained, "Sometimes the Gang gets a little wild. They might slosh hot cider on it. No use taking chances, okay, Dad?" He had nodded, but she could see it upset him.

"But Linda," Laurie explained as the two girls bicycled into the country to gather greens for decorations, "everyone in the Gang has a beautiful house, with oil paintings and sculpture and all that kind of stuff. Good quality. I'm really afraid they'd make fun of my father's Indian even if he does love it."

"But you were tactful, Laurie, and besides what you feared made good sense. I've got another idea. Want to borrow some of my mother's hanging houseplants? Then it will be all woodsy and different."

Mrs. Hudson didn't like the idea of not using the overhead lights, and she feared that candles could be dangerous.

"But, Mom, we want it mysterious and charming."

"It's too dark, too suggestive."

"Mom, you're gonna spoil it!" Laurie cried in dismay, but Tracy burst in with ideas.

"Hey, if you're gonna have a piñata you can have twisted crepe-paper ribbons all different colors."

Laurie hestitated. "We're not exactly ten years old."

But Linda interrupted. "A fabulous idea. I'll bet none of them ever did it. So even if you don't have a mansion, you've got originality. And we'd better get that piñata made, too. What colors shall we use?"

All in all, the preparations took on an air of festivity that was new in the Hudson house. Tracy was allowed to go with Linda and Laurie as they chose crepe paper — orange, red, yellow, purple, and a hot pink for the piñata and the twisted crepe streamers. They had decided to make a paper horse (although it came out looking like a vaguely defined four-legged animal, which could have also been a donkey or a goat), and they filled it with pieces of wrapped candy, some pennies, fortune cookies, a few old plastic rings, and Ping-Pong balls. By late Friday afternoon it hung from the ceiling while twisted ribbons of colored crepe branched out around it from wall to wall. The candles were ready to be lit, and the freshness of the pine and fir boughs had transformed the living room.

"Now, that's what I call a party," Mr. Hudson said, though he worried about the candles. Laurie swore she would be careful to watch them.

The mulled cider was bubbling in the kitchen, and the dining room table, covered with Mrs. Hudson's best cloth, would later hold the salads, the lasagna Mrs. Hudson had made, Linda's cheesecakes, and a chocolate cake. In the meanwhile, bowls of apples, corn chips, crackers, and cheese were placed here and there.

"Here," Laurie's mother said, giving her a box. "An early Christmas present for you. Go ahead, open it."

How Mrs. Hudson had managed to sew a silky, ruffled blouse and velvet pants, both of them in a delicious shade hovering between cherry and plum, Laurie did not know.

"Oh, Mom!" She threw her arms around her mother's neck. "It is so perfect! And exactly what's in style — oh, I love it!"

She put it on and her mother sighed in relief. "It's almost a perfect fit. The waist could still be tighter . . ."

"Mom, I'm really touched. I mean it —" Laurie's voice broke.

"Well, you don't give parties every day, so when you do, they should be perfect. And I hope . . . I hope for the best."

There, Laurie thought *she wants to say more but she can't.* In fact, a certain sentimentality seemed to fill the air. Mrs. Hudson said matter-of-factly, "Now, Bill and I will stay in the kitchen and see that there's enough cider and enough to eat and all that."

"I thought you were going out, not that I wouldn't want you here," Laurie stammered, fearing something might happen that would prove embarrassing. Some of the boys were sure to bring along whiskey or vodka. And if Alison should come . . .

She would take care of it when it happened. Thinking of Alison, she crossed her fingers, closed her eyes, and prayed silently and simply. "Please, please let this party happen as it should. It's so important!"

Everything was ready, and all she had to do was wait for the guests.

"Eight o'clock is much too early, even if it said so on the invitations," Laurie explained. But eight drifted slowly to eight-fifteen, eight-thirty, quarter-to-nine.

"They're always late. It's sophisticated," she explained to Tracy, who had to know why nobody came. But as nine o'clock grew closer, Laurie felt herself becoming pessimistic. Everything had been going wrong lately; why not this, too?

"What if they don't come at all?" Tracy asked loudly.

"Well then, we'll all drink cider and eat cheesecake and get fat and have a good time. Then we'll poke down the piñata and keep all the goodies," Mrs. Hudson said lightly, "but don't throw in the towel yet. I know they're going to come. Didn't you tell me once their parties usually start at ten?"

"Sure," Laurie said, going back into the living room where she sat by herself. She had lit two candles and they flickered lightly so that the strands of colored paper gleamed here and there. So pretty! Was she to sit here all night alone? No sooner had she decided the idea of a party had all been a mistake and it wasn't worth the torture of waiting than the doorbell rang loudly and everyone trooped in. Suddenly the party began. The house was filled with noise. Eddie and Mike carried a case of tapes, and Sally handed Laurie some chips and a dip as her contribution. Nobody had bothered to dress but wore whatever they had had on at school. Laurie alone appeared in party clothes, something else which set her apart, but at least some of the boys commented on it with what Laurie thought was genuine appreciation.

"Where were you all this time?" she asked.

"We all went out to Greeley's for pizza. Yum!"

A momentary stab of pain darkened the evening. They had all gone out and not asked her to join them. And she had told them there would be more than enough to eat at the party. *Let it go, Laurie, let it go. Not important.*

"Hey, this is really neat. Kind of like a jungle garden," someone said.

"I've never been here before. What I've missed! Marvelous plants."

"I like the decorations," Mike said as he pulled an orange crepe-paper ribbon, but he pulled too hard and it broke. He apologized.

"Anyone want some hot punch?" Laurie asked.

"So that's what it is. I'm full, but it smells great. What's in it anyway?"

"That's for you to figure out," Laurie said. She was moving among the guests and her face felt as though a smile had been painted on it. Bob had not come yet. Someone had put on some tapes at top volume and a few couples began to dance. In the corner of the room five jocks were talking about the Rose Bowl game and considering bets. Smoke began to fill the tiny room. It was not entirely unlike the usual parties, and yet the difference was unmistakable.

"Is that a real piñata?" someone asked. "I haven't had one of those since I was a kid."

"Yeah, this place has a nice party feeling," Mike said, and Laurie wondered if they meant it was too unsophisticated. Yet she smiled, offered more cider, made a point of talking with everyone lightly.

But Bob hadn't come. Had he decided to stay away?

Or . . . ? *Or what, Laurie?*

Her face was flushed and she felt disoriented. Someone was now playing a fast-paced rock and roll tape, and Jim Stowe grabbed her, practically commanding her to dance. She danced with the others and then as the song ended the front door opened and there stood Bob with Alison, hand in hand. Her head was thrown back as she glanced up at him, and both were laughing as though they were sharing a very funny joke. It wasn't their rudeness that hurt Laurie, but the way in which Bob looked at Alison. She recognized it instantly, knowing now that Bob was in love with Alison. She could no longer escape from the dreadful knowledge. The battle was lost. She stifled a moan of grief rising within her and stood by silently.

In seconds the grief turned to fury, for Bob could never be forgiven for bringing Alison. He must have known she had not been invited. Yet if she were to complain, Alison would leave with a great fuss, which would make Laurie appear mean and bitter. And so when Bob came over smiling broadly, she stiffened.

He drew her to him and kissed her. Laurie wanted to pull back, to lash out, but her pain was too new. It didn't matter anyway, for clearly this was not a kiss of love, but only the polite courtesy a guest gives his hostess.

The evening had hardly begun, yet it was over for Laurie. A proper hostess now with forced enthusiasm and a fixed smile, she saw to it that everyone had cider and held her tongue when she saw Sally and some of the boys touching up their grog with the Scotch they had. Nor did she say anything when the tape deck was turned up to deafening volume.

Now she had little to do but wait until it was over.

The floor cleared as Bob and Alison danced.

"Hey, everyone, watch this!"

"Fireworks. Those two! Wow!"

Bob danced well, turning and twisting while Alison, moving sinuously, her reddish hair falling flatteringly in her face, kept up with him easily. Immediately Laurie became busy in the kitchen and when she returned, that dance was over. Alison came up to Laurie to compliment her on the grog.

"It's so unusual and so mild. I love it. And your blouse is gorgeous. Everything here is so *cute*. Thanks for inviting me."

"I *didn't* invite you, Alison," Laurie said in a voice that only Alison could hear, and then she moved on, not wanting to make an issue of it. Alison, completely insensitive to the situation, winked at Bob and then kissed him as he poured some whiskey in her grog.

What are all these people doing? Laurie thought. She realized she didn't even like them very much. Michael and Gary asked her to dance and she did so, woodenly. Several girls began to pull at the crepe paper to see how far it would stretch and within a few minutes half the work of long preparation was undone as the colored strips dangled limply from the ceiling. In a corner several guests huddled to tell jokes, and once in a while a loud snort of laughter erupted from that tightly knit group.

Bob and Alison danced tirelessly, their eyes glued to one another.

When would this endless party be over?

Impatient though she was, it hurt even more when two girls, Sally and Lou, came up and said, "This was just the greatest party, Laurie. Thanks so much. It's really original, the piñata and everything. We're sorry, but we have to go."

"It's only ten-thirty," Laurie said.

"Yeah, but we're going skiing tomorrow, and we'll have to get up early and then back in time for a party, so do forgive us."

"Hey, Laurie, swell party but we have to go, too," Charlie said, and then everyone seemed to be putting on their jackets and crowding around Laurie, kissing her and telling her what a fantastic party it was.

"And that cheesecake is the *best*! Can I have one more smidgeon?" Alison cried, cutting a wedge and putting it in Bob's mouth while she finished the rest. *She's feeding him as if he were a pet — and he lets her,* Laurie thought.

"If everyone else is going, we may as well split, too," Bob said. "Laurie, aren't you proud? The party was a real success."

Lying only made it worse. Laurie had never felt more unable to talk or smile. She picked up the pile of tapes he had bought and put them in his arms.

"Want me to help you clear up?" Alison asked. The offer may have been genuine but

Laurie considered it an insult. "Bob, why don't we help Laurie?"

"No," she said in such a chilly voice that they backed off. She stood at the door stone-faced and rigid as Bob and Alison tumbled into the night with the rest of the party, laughing, punching one another playfully, and calling out good-byes until at last their talk and laughter became mingled with the roar of cars starting. Laurie watched the lights in back of the Dinky as it drove down the street and disappeared.

It was not quite eleven o'clock. The party for which Laurie had worked so hard and spent so much money lasted less than two hours. Paper strips hung from the ceiling, broken and limp, and the piñata, untouched, dangled gaily and mocked her with its innocent smile.

"Well, it was a great party! Thanks so much!" Laurie managed to beam and hug her mother.

"It was noisy enough, and that always means a good party," her mother said tactfully, keeping up the fiction. Fortunately, Tracy had gone to bed.

"There's so much food left over, and the piñata's still whole. Maybe you and Dad can have a party."

"Not us, but perhaps Tracy would like it. Maybe we ought to put the food away and blow out the candles. Want me to do it?"

"No, Mom, you've done so much. Let me do it, and then I'm off to bed."

Nevertheless, her mother helped her put away the food and then, understanding all too well what had happened, told Laurie to go to bed. The rest of it could be cleaned in the morning. Laurie promised she would do it all but admitted the party had tired her, so with a sweet good night, which took her last reserve of poise, she went to bed.

She wanted to sleep forever and never wake up.

Ten

The morning following the party, the house appeared as storm-wracked as Laurie felt. Red-eyed and pale, she tore off the pretty twisted lengths of crepe paper that hung limply where they had been teased and pulled. Cold as it was on that bleak December Saturday, Laurie had to open the windows to air the room — it had been impossible to keep anyone from smoking. Glasses were turned over and a puddle of cider glistened unpleasantly on the floor. There were crumbs everywhere, a broken cup, a half-eaten piece of cake on the coffee table that infuriated Laurie, for she had brought red paper napkins and had used her mother's best plates.

"Never mind," Mrs. Hudson said in a comforting way as she helped Laurie clear the mess.

"You don't have to lift a finger, Mom. It's all my fault. You were so nice to let me have this party and it cost so much and it turned out — well, it couldn't have been worse. Look at it. Oh, Mom, they were dreadful, weren't they? Pigs, all of them."

"Frankly, yes. That's how they behaved. Pigs would have been nicer."

"I never want to see any of them again. Not a single one."

Laurie could no longer keep back the tears.

"Darling, you don't have to. I know you're angry and disappointed, but it's not the end of the world. And it's better that you know it now. There are hundreds of other people you can get to know. I know you won't believe it, but they're waiting for you."

"Oh, Mom! You're such an optimist. Everything is over for me now. Everything." She was careful not to mention Bob's name, for that caused too much pain, but her mother, understanding, said nothing. She noticed, however, that for the first time Laurie no longer wore the gold football on its gold chain.

"At least the piñata is untouched. Look at it up there. It looks so happy."

"You will, too, one day, believe me, Laurie. And now, let's have some breakfast and then dig in."

While they made toast and coffee, Linda

came over to pick up her plants. Tactfully, Mrs. Hudson left them alone.

"It wasn't such a success, was it, Laurie? I can tell from your face. I'm sorry."

"Well, I gambled and I lost. That's it. Everything is over."

"You won't appreciate my saying this, Laurie, but frankly I don't think Bob was such a great bargain and it may be the best thing that Alison came along. Don't wince like that. Someday you'll understand."

"I loved him."

"See, you're using the past tense already. I guess this means you won't go to the Christmas Dance with him?"

"It doesn't seem that way. I simply won't go."

"You know Frank Lowry? He's got a thing for you. Why don't you go with him? He's very nice, a little short, but not bad-looking."

Laurie shook her head. "Thanks, but I'm not going to go at all. And that's that. Linda, please take home this cheesecake; they didn't get to it. And please let me give you some of the greens and . . ."

She helped Linda take back her mother's plants, and by early afternoon the Hudson living room was restored to its former self, homey and modest. Only the piñata remained to show that a party had been held there.

The last week of school dragged. Laurie walked through the halls, head held high, her manner reserved. If others gossiped, she paid no attention and didn't want to know.

It was the following Saturday night that she dreaded. Now she would become one of those lonely girls sitting before the TV while everyone else went to the Christmas Dance. Maybe she should put on her Homecoming tiara, she thought cynically, to show how popular she was.

Come on, now, stop this self-pity, her imaginary older sister scolded and she answered, *I would if only I could somehow wipe out Saturday night entirely.*

On Thursday of that week her answer came as she overheard Rita Santini complaining to a friend in the locker room at the end of gym class.

"Am I ever in a fix! You know I work at Pete's Pizza Palace down on Fourth Street. Well, I want to go to the Christmas Dance, and then the next day I'm supposed to go to Hawaii for the whole vacation. Lucky me, hey? Only if I don't find a substitute, I'll lose my job; Pete's real mad about my leaving during vacation. And I can't find anyone. Everyone's going to the dance."

Laurie turned to her. "Rita, if you like, I'll take your place. I'm not going to the dance, and I'll be here all vacation."

Please let me do it, she wanted to beg. More than anything she needed to be in a different place doing something she'd never done before.

"I've never worked in a restaurant, but I learn quickly."

"Laurie, you angel! Would you do this for me? Really?"

"Yeah, I would. I'd love to. Honest."

And then Rita, who had never said more than hello to Laurie, hugged her and cried, "You'll be perfect! Pete will adore you. Come on and I'll tell you all about it.

"You'll make fantastic tips," she said as she wiggled neatly into her jeans and shirt. "You can wear my uniform. We're about the same size. And now, this is what you have to do . . ."

The girls walked down the hall together and then, just before they parted, Rita blinked as if she thought of something. "How come you're not going to the dance? Weren't you going around with Bob?"

To her surprise, Laurie laughed. Here she had always thought everyone in the school considered her and Bob as the Lovers and Rita — who got around if anyone did — was hardly aware of it.

"Something like that," she answered, for after all she didn't have to explain anything to anyone. "But I'm not going to the dance, and I'll love working at Pete's. And that's just how it is!"

"Sure. It's not bad. You'll love it," Rita said, then the girls had to rush to class.

Two things had happened then. She would most likely have a real job that would help her pay off the debts she owed — those dreadful debts — and she encountered the first person who had asked about Bob and she had tossed off the question without bursting into tears.

Tiny, tiny victories — if anything can be a victory to a girl with a broken heart, which was how Laurie thought of herself.

Eleven

All that week Laurie felt as though her face were carved out of wood, and it was still that way on Saturday at five-thirty when she showed up at Pete's Pizza Palace. Still, she managed to put on the required smile. She was relieved of one fear: the Gang never went to Pete's although it was every bit as good as those pizza parlors miles away where they usually went. So they would not see her waiting on tables the night of the dance.

"Well, I'm glad Rita found a nice girl like you. You'll do fine, and you'll make good money. Remember, good service is what you have to think about. Okay, we'll take it easy this first night, but I warn you, we'll be busy."

Pete, a large, dark-haired man with a vast,

pizza-filled frontage, grinned at Laurie, patted her shoulder, and instructed her about the tables she was to cover, what had to be done, and how she should behave. Then Laurie changed to Rita's uniform of white shirt, black skirt, and a red-and-white striped apron, folk-loric and peasantry, a little too sweet, but on the whole charming. When she came out of the dressing room Pete gave her a tiny red rosebud.

"Pin it in your hair. It's a holiday touch. Perfect!" Pete said in a hoarse, whispery voice that reminded Laurie of *The Godfather*. The restaurant with its candles in chianti bottles and red-checked tablecloths and artificial grape-vines decorating the walls had created a for-eign atmosphere, which to Laurie seemed perfect. She needed something different.

The evening began slowly. Pete introduced her to the chefs, the busboys, and the other waitresses. Then she began, ever so timidly, waiting on the first customers. Almost immedi-ately another couple came in to sit in the back corner where she had been assigned. It took concentration to remember to bring water, to know which table wanted the big pizza with everything, which wanted two medium pizzas, one with anchovies and hold the cheese on the other. She also had to remember who wanted coffee and who wanted beer and so on. Yet all this made it possible for her to forget the Christmas Dance and Bob; why, she real-ized when she took her five-minute break, that for two whole hours she hadn't given him a single thought.

The tips amazed her. Although they would have to be shared with the busboys, they added up rapidly, and she figured that during the time she replaced Rita she would have paid off that foolish but lovely sweater she had bought so rashly, would have repaid her mother for part of the expensive dress she had worn at Homecoming, and would be able to find Christmas presents for her parents and Tracy.

Yet just as she found herself grateful for this stroke of good luck, a young couple walked in and sat together closely at a table, the way she and Bob used to sit together. Suddenly all the pain blocked her spirits as she relived all the misery of the last month. She tortured herself by imagining Bob and Alison dancing together under the blinking fairy-tale lights that had been set up around the gym where the Christmas Dance took place. She was seized with an impulse to cry, but then someone called to her, "Miss, Miss, may we have some dessert? What would you suggest?" She hurried to the table to take the order and was jolted out of the tricks of her imagination.

About nine-thirty, as her legs began to ache, Pete pointed to a table by the window. "The couple at table thirteen is ready to order."

"Okay, I'll get to them," she said, and then nearly choked, for it was Gregory Munson who sat there, looking slightly unfamiliar in a dark suit, shirt, and tie. A girl was with him, the same one Laurie had seen with him at the concert. It was curious that she resembled him so, being tall and slender with the same proud posture and easy-moving grace, intense dark eyes, black thick hair, and a slight ruddiness under the olive skin. So that was Greg's girl, was it? How ridiculous for Laurie to find herself wishing she were in her place, when Greg hardly even said hello to Laurie. She could not tell if they had gone to the dance or not, for certainly they wouldn't have left it so quickly. Whatever — she'd better give them her friendly smile and pleasant "good evening."

Greg was studying the menu as she approached, but blinked when he looked up and saw Laurie there.

"Well, what are *you* doing here? I've never seen you here before."

"I've just begun to work tonight. I'm substituting for a friend."

"I thought surely you'd be at the dance. Aren't you the original party girl?"

"Where on earth did you get that idea? Not at all. Were you at the dance?"

"Jean and I went over for a little while, but we left. We don't care too much about it, do we, Jean?"

"Actually I do care about it, Greg, when you're not stepping all over my feet and I'm not stepping all over yours." She finished with a wide, charming grin, and Laurie could see why Greg liked her. *Was he in love with her?* she wondered. If only someone loved her, she would be happy, so happy. Then she heard Pete cough warningly, and so she became the waitress once more.

"What would you like? If you're not ready to order, I'll come back in a few minutes."

In the meanwhile she had to go to the kitchen and wait while the salads were being prepared for another table. From that distance Laurie watched them discussing the menu. She knew so little about Greg, had never seen him with a girl before the concert, but she had watched him almost every day as he dashed through the halls as though he couldn't bear to walk slowly. They shared a math class and an English class, and he seemed brilliant. He wasn't always well liked because he brought up controversial issues and could be blunt, but he was never rude. He earned respect, no doubt of that, but not the crude popularity that Bob had cultivated. It had always bothered Laurie that Bob disliked Greg. Laurie had never agreed with Bob, although she had kept quiet about it. Now she realized she could think whatever she liked.

Laurie took their order and brought them their pizza but could not linger because a dozen students, who most likely had just left the Christmas Dance, walked in, talking noisily and laughing uproariously at some joke. The girls wore vivid colors, reds, purples, and gleaming whites; their hair had been curled and cared for; their makeup generously applied. As a group they took on a certain gaudy, jungle-flower beauty.

Pete nudged her. "They'll probably want two tables together, and Bill will help you. Just ask him."

Laurie turned around in time to see Greg and Jean leaving. Greg turned his head, looked at her directly, then nodded and left. *At least he knows I'm alive*, she thought, and then turned toward the laughing crowd that was now being seated.

Fearing that they would recognize her, she kept as impersonal a profile as she could manage, and then didn't know whether to be relieved or hurt because they did not seem to know her. Perhaps it was better that they thought her an anonymous waitress. However, as she brought in the jumbo pizza they had ordered, one of the girls stared at her, snapping her fingers as if trying to recall something.

"Say, aren't you . . . aren't you . . . the Homecoming Queen?"

"Sure! You're Laurie Hudson, aren't you?" the girl in the cerise strapless dress asked.

"I guess I am!" Laurie said, lightly and pleasantly, as she placed the pizza on the table.

"Well, what are you doing here? I mean, after all . . ." a girl in a wild, printed dress blurted out, as though she couldn't believe it. The boy who sat beside her poked her with his elbow, and Laurie saw him whisper something that most likely was an order to shut up. The implication could not have been more clear. Homecoming Queens do not wait on tables at Pete's on the night of the Christmas Dance, but Laurie smiled so agreeably as she asked what they would drink, that it would seem as if she preferred doing this to going to a dance.

Back in the kitchen as she waited for an anchovy pizza to come out of the oven, she leaned against the white tile wall feeling as though someone had forced her eyes open and said, "Take a good look, Laurie. Face the truth."

She could not deny the joy of being chosen, elected by the school for what had seemed the most honored place. Now the glory of it evaporated like a soap bubble, for it had lasted for one night and then died.

"Table ten, pizza with anchovies . . ." the chef's tired voice rang out.

Laurie's arms were ready to fall off and her feet ached, yet she picked up the tray with its steaming pizza and delivered it, actually *smiling* as she did so.

At last the evening was over for her, her shift ending at midnight. Pete came over to her. "You're okay, Laurie. I've been watchin' you. For a first night, you done fine."

"Thanks, thanks very much."

"You'll come back tomorrow? Can I depend on you?"

"Oh, yes!"

Not a great victory, but another victory nevertheless, she thought as she changed into her jeans and sweater. Someone wanted her. Pete thought she was good.

Her father was waiting in front of Pete's in their secondhand Toyota, the family car. Laurie collapsed in the seat beside him.

"You're sure tired, aren't you? Laurie, you don't have to do this, you know. We're getting along fine."

"It's okay. I like it."

"Did you eat lots of pizza?" Mrs. Hudson asked when Laurie hobbled into the kitchen.

"I'm cured of it forever. I didn't eat anything. There wasn't time. But I'm making money. About time, isn't it?"

"It helps. And now let me get you a late snack and then maybe you ought to take a hot bath," Mrs. Hudson said. She fed Laurie hot chocolate and buttered toast — childhood food — as if Laurie were a little girl. But it comforted Laurie, as did this familiar kitchen with her mother sitting at the table talking and working on a crossword puzzle and her father reading the sports page of the early-edition Sunday paper.

"Home is really good," she said, petting Patch as he jumped up for a corner of toast.

Nobody said a word about the Christmas Dance and she thought, *Thank heavens it's over and I don't have to fear it anymore*. She rested in the hot, soapy bath and could have wept privately over Bob. But she found herself thinking instead of Gregory Munson. So he had thought her a party girl, but she wasn't that, not really, even though she had gone to ever so many of the Gang's parties. And now those were over where she was concerned. What lay ahead she could not tell. Only that Gregory Munson was an interesting person. Interesting.

*T*welve

Patch, that peculiar, shaggy, fifty-seven-variety dog that the Hudsons had rescued from the ASPCA, walked with Laurie out toward the hills, those lonely heights on the edge of town, so golden in summer and now in the dead of winter, gray. When the rains came they would turn brown, but the rains were late that year. Laurie sat on a rock and confided in Patch.

"Patch, it's really awful, so awful. I miss Bob so much. How can he do this to me?"

Patch wagged his tail sympathetically and licked her face. He became her confessor, listening carefully to everything she had to say and promising never to reveal it.

"Everyone else is having a marvelous vacation. Nobody calls me. Linda would, but she's gone to L.A. with her mother. Even the girls in the Gang — Sally, Teri, maybe Valerie — they seemed nice, they came to my party, but now that Bob has someone else it's as if I've never existed."

Laurie hated her self-pity, and yet she had to let it out. Patch snuggled up against her as if to say that he was there and it was all right for her to say what she felt.

"I'm getting educated fast, Patch. Bob can't possibly love me anymore, and now I wonder if he ever did. Yes, he did at one time. And I thought I was popular, what a joke. Wow, Patch, I thought I was the luckiest girl in the world. Some luck!"

But then she patted Patch and held him close, ashamed to lay such negative emotions on such a little dog. Besides, she had to get ready for work, so she got up and raced him home.

The vacation dragged. Surprisingly enough she found herself happier at Pete's than anywhere else, for there she had to concentrate on being friendly, but not too friendly; her outside life had to be put aside while she worked; so she saved her private grief for that blessed time when she would go home and crawl into bed. Exhausted, she slept well, but then, she could not sleep forever.

If only they could skip Christmas that year — but one does not skip that climactic holiday. The family wrapped presents, trimmed the

tiny tree, and listened to carolers who sere-
naded them and accepted the cookies Tracy
and Mrs. Hudson had made.

On Christmas morning the family ex-
changed presents. Always on other Christmas
mornings Bob would come over with gifts for
the family, usually a large fruitcake or a box
of cheeses, and something personal for Laurie.
She had bought a soft, crimson scarf for him
this year just in case he came over, but it remained unseen in its tissue wrappings at the
bottom of her drawer. He would not come this
Christmas.

But Mr. Hudson would not let Laurie remain quiet as the family sat among the boxes
and heaps of paper. He presented her with a
box.

"Laurie, it's just what you need. Guess what
it is!"

Laurie shook the box. "I can't. C'mon, Dad,
don't tease."

Had her father bought clothes for her? But
he knew nothing about her taste — absolutely
nothing. The family watched as Laurie opened
the box and picked up a blue sweat shirt and
pants for winter running, a sleeveless vest and
shorts for warmer days, and blue-and-white
Nike running shoes in her size. The card said,
"TO HELP THOSE TIRED LEGS OF YOURS, LOVE,
DAD."

"What a real surprise! Dad, this is great. But
I'm not a runner."

"I know, but you should be. I'd like to see

you jogging, building yourself up. It's a good thing to do."

"This is a beautiful outfit," Laurie said, realizing it must have cost a considerable sum. "I'll have to try it on. Right now!"

"I might even get myself an outfit and go jogging with you, Laurie. We'd become perfect physical specimens. How about it, Laurie girl?"

"Oh, Dad, you're such a daring!" Laurie hugged him and then sat on his lap, big as she was. He patted her shoulder as though she were a little girl who had skinned her knee playing. Thoughtful as he was, however, his eyes remained glued on the TV as he watched an important football game. For all his sweetness and good intentions, Laurie knew little chance existed for a morning jog with her father.

I'll go jogging tomorrow, she promised herself.

Stop thinking about the past, stupid! her imaginary, unsympathetic big sister told her. Yet Laurie, helping her mother in the kitchen, could not help but think about past Christmas vacations when Laurie was always invited to the Hamiltons' cabin at Squaw Valley, which was really a redwood house. Even though Mrs. Hamilton was always subtly critical, Laurie had borne it sweetly as long as she and Bob could go up in the lift and see the white world and the pointed, green pines below. At first she had been afraid to ski, but Bob, an excellent coach, taught her so that she graduated from the easy slopes to the steeper, more demanding ones. Skiing became a passion. She loved being there, watching the other skiers in their bright clothes, silhouetted against the snow and the sky, which could be brilliant blue or pale blue or dove gray as it filled with huge, moist snowflakes.

That was another world, and now she was cast out of it and living in a cold and lonely December-gray Edgewood. One afternoon Laurie took a long walk with Patch through the quiet streets, brightened only by sparkling Christmas lights that blinked with what seemed to Laurie to be desperate good cheer.

"Laurie, telephone. You'll never guess who!"

"Don't shout, Tracy. Your voice carries," Laurie whispered fiercely, wondering who it could be. Bob?

"Hello?" she asked uncertainly.

"Hi, love! How are you?" Bob, it *was* Bob! Her heart leaped. A ghost had come back.

"Great. And you?"

"Getting along. Fabulous vacation, isn't it? We've all been up at Squaw, had Christmas there. Laurie, want to go to San Francisco with me? There's a great football movie I want to see, and we can go out to dinner to this new Chinese restaurant that is supposed to be super."

"Thanks, Bob." Laurie hesitated, holding the phone close to her as though it were a love object. Was he coming back to her then? Bob, less than verbal about personal emotions, would chose to do it in just this way, but still that auburn-haired girl floated between them as clearly as though she lay curled up in the telephone wires.

"What about Alison?" Laurie asked as lightly as she could, hoping, hoping so much that that fling was over.

"She can't go," he said, so obviously he had already asked her. "She had a row with her folks, who wanted her to go to Sun Valley. You can't blame her for wanting to go there. So here I am."

So now Laurie was to be second fiddle? Never.

"Thanks for asking, Bob, but I think I'll pass it up."

"You have something else on? C'mon, I thought you liked going to the city. You love Chinese food, don't you?"

Dumb, dumb Bob. Did she have to spell it out?

"Bob, think about the total situation. Think real hard," Laurie said, possibly with too much scorn in her voice, so she softened her tone. "I've really got to go. I'm going out, so thanks for calling, Bob. See you around."

"Well, if that's how you feel . . ." He was insulted, his feelings hurt. For a few moments the telephone held them together, though neither of them spoke. This was good-bye.

Farewell. The end. Did Bob understand? The quality of his voice changed, becoming low and thoughtful but determined.

"Well, since the movie will be around for a while, I'll just wait until Alison gets back since you're so busy. She'll want to see it."

"That's fine with me, Bob. So long."

"*Ciao.*"

Laurie cried a little, but the message could not have been clearer. The last good-bye had been said. She swathed the gold football in tissue and put it back in the white pasteboard jeweler's box it came in. She wrapped it in plain brown paper and addressed it to Bob. No note, no last tender words, no bitter accusations. Nothing.

Before she could lose her nerve, she put on her jacket and scarf and walked briskly to the post office. The clerk weighed the package and called out the postage in a bored voice. Laurie paid it, watched the clerk stamp the box and throw it into the huge mail cart. There, the deed was done.

Good-bye, Bob, good-bye.

Yet as Laurie stepped out into the chilling gray air again, she felt strangely lighter. The great love affair was finished, over, kaput! Happiness was far out of reach, but freedom was something else. Suddenly dizzy with her liberation, she could not bear to walk but instead ran through the streets back home.

Thirteen

New Year's Eve. For the first time Laurie stayed home alone to welcome the new year. Her parents reluctantly kissed her good night as they went to a neighborhood party, and popular Tracy had waved good-bye gaily and gone off to a pajama party with friends.

"I'll be fine," Laurie insisted. "I've got Patch and a new mystery novel I've been dying to read for ages."

No more self-pity. She resolved not to think of Bob, not to think of parties everywhere, but plunged resolutely into the murder mystery. Patch curled up beside her, and she could almost forget what night it was until the high-pitched cries of a dozen little girls' voices — Tracy's among them — cried, "Happy New

Year" to everyone. A clatter of pans and lids sounded through the quiet streets.

"Happy New Year," "Happy New Year," "Happy New Year!"

Laurie bent over and kissed Patch but wondered if she would ever be happy again.

Only one resolution forced itself upon Laurie. She would have to go jogging, or her father's feelings would be hurt forever. At six A.M. on January first, she put on her running outfit and found herself delighted with its soft, fleecy feel and its lovely color, a rich royal blue with white stripes down the sides. At least her clothing pleased her, but what did she know about running or jogging? Nothing. Absolutely nothing. It was unlikely that anyone would see her at dawn on January first. The streets were empty, not even a dog in sight. In the east, horizontal bands of color celebrated a cool yet radiant winter dawn.

Laurie began to run along a route she had sketched for herself through the old residential section of Edgewood where Bob had lived when he first moved to town, past the school campus, and up a hill from which the surrounding landscape could be seen, and from there back down to the flat, dull streets of East Edgewood where she lived.

Not bad, she thought for the first few blocks and then her side began to ache, her legs hurt, and she struggled for breath. She slowed down and stopped entirely, waiting for her breath to return. She had heard of runners going on for hours and hours — or was it days and days? — without getting winded, but not for a moment did she believe it.

Still the streak of stubbornness that appeared now and then in the Hudson family emerged in full force, and so Laurie continued. Five more blocks and then a turn up one of those tree-lined hills that made Edgewood such a pretty place. Yet this hill, gentle as it was, took on the aspects of Mt. Everest as Laurie pushed upward, her face a steamy red and her breath coming with difficulty. Nevertheless, she made it to the top of the hill, and there she saw another runner in the distance. *A real runner,* she thought, legs stretching ahead of him easily and rhythmically, strong and yet delicate like the legs of a racehorse. As he came closer, running uphill much faster than Laurie could go downhill, she saw a flash of red, a headband. And then she could see that this was Greg Munson, out for a morning dash.

Not now, she cried with anguish. She could not bear for anyone to see her in her present condition, hair tangled and her mouth open as she gasped for breath like a fish out of water. She had never looked worse, and here was Greg Munson, of all people, running up the hill.

Seeing her, he raised his eyebrows as if to say, well, what have we here? It was exactly the same look he had given her the night he'd seen her in Pete's Pizza. Amused? Surprised? Laurie smiled at him weakly, and as he ran past her he nodded his head slightly to acknowledge that he saw her.

Is he laughing at me? Laurie wondered.

"I'll show him," Laurie said out loud. If she did nothing else in her life, even if it meant an early death, she would let him know that she could run. She would not be put down, not by him or anyone.

Still, home seemed miles away although it was only six blocks. Again she became breathless and her legs ached. Would she really have to go through this torture day after day after day?

At last she limped home and collapsed on a chair as her father was getting up. He chucked her under the chin and said, "Out for a run? That's my girl!"

"Your girl? I'm a breathless wreck."

Nevertheless, as she showered she found herself singing. She'd show Greg Munson with his raised eyebrows and disapproving grin. *Just wait!*

*F*ourteen

Improvement, if it came at all, would come slowly, she feared. The second morning's run found her as exhausted as the first, yet she held her head high, sure that she'd cross Greg Munson's path again. Or would he chose a different route to avoid seeing her?

It was like picking petals from a daisy. He'd come, he'd stay away, he'd come . . . and so forth. It kept Laurie running long after she wanted to stop on that second day. This time he came earlier or she was running slower, for as she pushed her reluctant legs up the hill, he arrived on the summit. A day of morning sun caught the burnished dark of his hair and lit the edges of the red headband as he loped along, graceful and tireless as a deer. Running can be so beautiful, Laurie realized as she watched him.

But she didn't know how to do it. Something must be wrong in the way she went about it. But her stubborn streak sent her running faster than she believed possible *up* the hill. This time Greg did not raise his eyebrows in surprise or disapproval but shook his head almost imperceptibly as if to ask, "What on earth do you think you're doing? Running?"

School began on January third. She continued to jog, although she would have preferred to stay in bed. The damp fog was rolling in, so sometimes the air was clear and other times opaque, so that she seemed to be running through a cloud. The calves of her legs still ached and she groaned, "Oh, Lord, why me?" But she continued to run anyway.

Like the other two mornings, this one held a question. Would Greg be there? Yes, there he was! She could see his handsome form rising above the summit of the hill and, determined to show him she would not be defeated, she sprinted forward, panting and red-faced. A dog barked, then suddenly crossed her path, an ungainly red setter. Laurie stumbled and fell, cursing her awkwardness. Immediately Greg Munson kneeled beside her.

"Are you hurt?"

"I'm embarrassed. I didn't see that dog." Laurie stood up and rubbed the dust from her new sweat shirt.

"In this fog things like that happen. You're sure you're okay?" He asked this kindly, without being overly solicitous. At least he did not laugh at her as Bob would have done, nor did he move away, but simply stood there, regarding her seriously.

"You realize, don't you, that you're not running correctly? I can point out at least five things that are wrong with your technique."

"Why not make it six things or an even dozen?" Laurie answered flippantly, feeling that everything she did was wrong. But he paid no attention to the remark.

"I take it you're new at this, and you haven't been trained, have you?"

"No."

"Okay. You need some help, or you'll only end up hating running and that would be a shame because it's a great thing to do. In the first place, you're trying to go too fast. Speed and distance should be the least of your worries right now. So take it easy. Feel the rhythm of it. You don't have to run a marathon next week, you know."

Unexpectedly he grinned. A friendly grin. And she wanted to thank him for relieving her of the need to show off.

"At first it will seem as if you have to watch lots of things — your breathing, the way your legs move, your arms — but don't worry. One day it will all come together.

"You want to have a better posture. Hold your head up and your shoulders down; don't let them hunch up. That's it. Two more things for now: Your legs are going off to the sides as if you were wearing a tight skirt. Your calves probably hurt but you'll get over that soon enough. Move from your hips as if you were running along a track two feet wide. Okay? Your arms are going out here and there like a windmill — no wonder you get winded. If you use your arms right, they'll help you run faster. Keep them closer to your body; make a gentle fist, thumbs out. Relax your wrists but don't let them flop. Like this."

He spoke simply and with authority. Then suddenly he smiled, a frank, friendly grin that surprised Laurie — he had dimples. How charming!

"You don't have to be embarrassed, Laurie. Everyone, almost everyone, begins like this or a lot worse. Want to run with me for a while?"

He touched her elbow lightly, a professional tap indicating she should hold her arms closer to her body, but even so, excitement rippled through her veins, clearly an unprofessional thrill that had little to do with running.

Then they ran together lightly and easily with no need of hurrying. Greg's body worked in perfect coordination. Laurie could see that clearly now; she found also that being close to him, sensing his rhythm, almost transmitted his ease of running to her.

They ran silently, but from time to time he corrected her. "Your left leg should be straighter. Good, that's it!"

128

Once he stopped and placed his hands on her shoulders. "Why are you so tense? Are you worried about something? There, relax, let them fall naturally. Feel the difference?"

They ran. Now and then he turned to her as if to say, "See how easy it is, how simple, how pleasant!" He ran with her over the course she had set and when they came to her house, she stopped.

"Thanks so much, Greg," she said, still winded, so she spoke in a breathless way. "I have to get ready for school, but you helped me a lot."

"Fine," he said, and in the next second he was bounding away, truly running this time, his long legs stretching out easily in front of him. In a twinkling he disappeared from view. She wondered if he liked her, or was it simply so painful to him to see her running badly that he had to interfere? It went without saying that he taught her well. Oh, yes, she had really loved running this time — or was this because he had run beside her?

"Whatever!" she sang loudly in the shower and then got ready for school. But then the old fears haunted her.

What would happen when she saw Bob and Alison together? Would she scream or kick Bob or tear Alison's hair? And would the girls in the Gang talk with her? Would those other girls in school who had been jealous make snide remarks? Whatever happened, there could be no comparison between school now and school as it was not so very long ago, a place where she felt herself queen.

Nevertheless, that morning run with Greg gave her courage in a way she could not explain. At least someone cared for her even if it were only a kindness on his part and nothing more.

She walked to school, head high and, remembering Greg's advice, shoulders down. Oddly enough, this very slight change gave her courage. And then she walked through the knot of seniors standing outside the main door of the school.

"Hi, Laurie, how are you?" Sally and Teri came forward toward her and she could read the sympathy in their eyes. A double realization hit her as she sensed that they seemed to care, but at the same time knew it wasn't sympathy that she wanted.

"I'm fine!" she said with an enthusiasm that may have surprised them. "And how about you?"

They murmured an answer, and she walked on. In some mysterious way they, as well as the rest of the Gang, had taken on the aspects of the past tense, something that happened before. They were outgrown, like clothes that had become too small. *What a strange reaction*, Laurie thought. But the test she dreaded would come when she saw Bob and Alison.

Since a new schedule had begun, she had no idea if they would share classes with her, and apparently this was not about to happen. She did not see them until after lunch as they walked down the hall, holding hands and gazing at one another.

This was the scene she had feared, the one that would shake her emotions like an earthquake. And what happened was that nothing happened at all. They seemed entirely self-centered and even a little silly. Yet Laurie had to confess it hurt even so; but if it ached, it was the pain of a wound that was being healed.

It was the sight of another couple embracing at the foot of the stairs that stopped her short with a longing so intense it was nearly painful. She wanted someone to love her, someone she could love. Not Bob, for that was finished. But someone.

Greg? Yes, but there was that girl, Jean. Stop dreaming, Laurie, sounded the wise, but imaginary, older sister. *You'll only get hurt all over again.*

Laurie hurried to her next class, and on the way she noticed a red sign on the bulletin board.

TRYOUTS FOR CHORUS WILL BE HELD ON WEDNESDAY AFTER SCHOOL IN THE MUSIC ROOM. APPLICANTS WILL SING A SONG OF THEIR CHOICE AND WILL BE ASKED TO SIGHT-READ.

Laurie read the announcement again and, without realizing it, memorized the time and place of the tryouts. When she had heard the Christmas concert she had wanted nothing more than to be part of the chorus. And here was the opportunity.

Come on, Laurie, don't make a fool of your-self! her cautious big sister warned. The advice made good sense. She could hardly read music at all. And what songs did she know other than the cheers? She could not very well "rah, rah, team!" her way into chorus. Of course, she did know a few folk songs; perhaps she could pre-pare one of those.

Stop dreaming, Laurie! Everyone would be trying out and the chorus was limited to twenty-four voices. It was no secret that some students took voice lessons and even had professional careers in mind. So what chance did she have?

Nothing was more ridiculous than for her to think of getting in, and yet hope fastened itself to her and would not let go.

Fifteen

When Laurie got home, Tracy was playing with friends in the living room, so she pulled out a tattered book of songs, which had always been on the bookshelf, and went to her bedroom. What kind of voice did she have? Soprano? Alto? She scarcely knew. At least cheerleading had demanded that she use her voice, and use it she did, developing substantial volume. But singing was something else again.

Laurie practiced scales and then opened the song book to the few songs she did know: "Red River Valley," "On Top of Old Smoky," a few others. Where she had learned them, she couldn't remember, but they were songs she loved. She tried to relate the tunes to the black dots with their tiny flags on the five-lined staff but remained baffled. What did sharps mean? What on earth were the flats she had heard about? It would be like learning a whole new language to distinguish one note from another. Some were thickly clustered and black, while others were fat, open circles, and still others were bracketed together with a tiny three on top. She would never learn. Never.

Sitting on the edge of the bed, Laurie thought she was a failure — in every way. She ran poorly. Her schoolwork was hardly brilliant; she was scarcely passing. The blow from Bob had hurt her deeply, and she still wept over his loss once in a while. Could she risk another failure?

In the past she had succeeded in almost everything she'd tried because she was careful not to attempt too much and to stay away from anything at which she might fail.

Yet she loved music, and if by chance she did get in, she would be in the chorus for nearly six months. Did she dare try?

Lying on the bed, she glanced up at the ceiling as though the answer would be written there. Nothing was written, but an image flickered — Greg running beside her.

He had been meeting her every morning, running silently beside her, often changing their course so that they ran through different parts of Edgewood. He only spoke to remind her of some small technical matter she should watch for. Although Laurie found her curiosity growing about him, she saw that the quietness seemed to bring them closer together in some way that had nothing to do with words. From time to time he caught her eye, and she thought he sometimes nodded his head slightly as if to say everything was fine or she was doing well or it was good to be running together early in the morning.

Now, lying on her bed, she had a vision of Greg smiling at her and saying, "Go ahead, try out. Have faith in yourself. You have to take chances, because if you don't, what else is there?"

The wind hammered at the window and Laurie shivered. Is this what her life had become, a succession of chilly, dismal days in which she stayed home with nothing to look forward to? There had to be something more.

"Of course! Now you're catching on!" Greg seemed to say.

Foolish Laurie, imagining such things. Right at the moment Greg was probably out with that pretty girl, Jean. And yet she was almost sure that's what he *would* have said had he been with Laurie.

All right then! She had a week in which to prepare for the tryout. Standing up now, she picked up the songbook and turned to "Red River Valley," which she knew by heart. Slowly she related the tune she knew to the black notes, and little by little, she began to see how the written music compared to the melody she knew. Yet much of it remained a mystery.

What if the song were too simple, too folksy? Still, it was as lovely a song as she knew, and so she sang it again and again until her voice grew tired and she had to stop. Besides, her mother had just come home from work and Laurie wanted to help her make dinner.

"What are you so happy about?" her mother asked as Laurie prepared a salad, but Laurie only shook her head.

Yet the song seemed to sing itself within her. She would try out, but it would remain a secret. It would be something new, something exciting, and, for Laurie, something chancy and dangerous.

On the day of the tryouts Laurie entered the Music Room and found it already filled with students waiting to try their luck. The secretary took down her name.

"They should have numbers, like in the delicatessen!" someone shouted.

Two girls walked over to the secretary and asked her to cross out their names. "We're leaving. There are only eleven places open and about a hundred and eleven trying to get in. No use waiting."

Three boys and then two more girls left, but Laurie remained. A boy with a bass voice stood next to her and practiced the music he prepared while two sopranos, practicing with trills and flutterings, were good enough for opera, or so Laurie thought. She caught a glimpse of the music they were singing and it was so complicated compared to the simple music she had chosen. But she thought she would try out anyway, even though with every moment that passed her confidence shrank.

One by one each candidate was called to one of the smaller performance rooms where Mr. Rappaport sat at the piano; though everyone strained to hear, the thick, well-designed door allowed nothing to escape. The candidates left through another door so they couldn't report what it was like.

Speculation ran high. "Carmen'll get in. She sang solos in church, and you can't believe how good she is."

"Susie Johnson is just as good. She's already got a job singing."

"I'll bet on Carmen."

"He's already got all the sopranos he needs; it's basses and tenors he wants," one of the boys said.

Bets were not actually made, but still there were rumors. The door opened for a second when the secretary gave a message to Mr. Rappaport, and the high, rich, fluttery sounds of Carmen's voice poured into the room where a crowd still waited.

"How can we compete with *that?*" someone cried.

Why wait? Laurie wondered. It would be so easy to cross her name off the list and not bother with the humiliation that waited for her. How could "Red River Valley" possibly compare with what she had just heard? Yet no sooner did she decide to leave than the secretary called her name from the list.

"Is Laurie Hudson still here?"

Nervously, Laurie walked into the room, where Mr. Rappaport, letting his fingers play along the piano keys in a bright and sparkling run, smiled at her.

"Laurie Hudson, I've seen you before. Wait, wait, I'll get it. On the field. You were one of the cheerleaders, weren't you? Now that's using your voice. Did you prepare something for today?"

" 'Red River Valley.' I hope it's all right."

"Of course it's all right. What's wrong with it? A lovely song. Don't be so frightened, Laurie. Here, want me to accompany you on the first verse?"

"Yes, please."

He made it easy for her, playing so beautifully and softly that after a false, quavery start, he stopped her and said, "Let's begin again." This time she sang out, and unexpectedly, the real beauty of the song became clear. Although it was sentimental, it was a song about farewells, sad and inevitable. Laurie could not be sure about the exact timing of the song and so sang it only as she had heard it, yet in a deep, inner way she knew what she was singing. Mr. Rappaport stopped playing and let her sing the second verse alone, and then, surprisingly enough, he allowed her to sing the third.

"Very, very nice," he said when she was finished. "You sing with a fine natural directness in your voice, and there's lots of power there; but you haven't sung much, have you, in church choir or anything?"

"No."

"Let's try a little sight-reading. Here's the second soprano part of a motet. It's a medieval hymn. It goes like this."

He handed her the music and played a few measures. She might just as well have handed it back to him, for she couldn't read it. But she listened carefully to what he played and more or less got the drift of it. Even so, it was ludicrous for Laurie to sing when he asked her to begin. The first few measures went well, but at one point he stopped her.

"That's an *F* sharp there. You have to hold it for three beats. Let's try again."

It made no sense to Laurie, and she confessed, "I can't read the music."

"But you just sang some of it."

"I listened to you play it."

And so, Laurie thought, *it's all over.* "Thanks for letting me try out."

"Wait a minute. Don't go. You don't read music?"

He tapped impatiently with his long, slender fingers as if he was thinking. Then he asked,

"Can you sing a scale — *do*, *re*, *mi*, and so on?"

"Yes."

He played a note. "This is *do*. Up and down the scale, all right?"

He tested her on several different scales. "Laurie, I believe you have perfect pitch. That's relatively rare."

She didn't know what perfect pitch was but was pleased that it delighted Mr. Rappaport so much.

"Laurie, I doubt that you'll make it to grand opera, but if you work hard enough, you may become a very nice little singer. But you're going to have to read music. It's not impossible, but it takes work. Would you be willing to learn, say within two weeks, if someone were to teach you?"

"Yes, I'd love it."

"Well, I'll consider that. You have a lot of catching up to do, you know. Thanks for coming. The names will be posted at the end of the week on the bulletin board."

He opened the far door for her and smiled enigmatically. Laurie left, not knowing whether she had made chorus or not, but she had tried. More important than that, with Mr. Rappaport playing she felt as though she had *discovered* music. It meant more to her now than she had ever dreamed. Another language!

She got home, hardly knowing what to do with this new emotion. Certainly she could not sit down in her room and begin homework. On an inspiration Laurie put on her running pants and sweat shirt and moving into an easy rhythm, slipped lightly over the path that led to the park. Although the air was chilly, a new warmth surged through her and she hardly noticed that this time her legs did not ache as she ran, nor did she become winded.

Two days later, keeping her fingers crossed, she approached the bulletin board. *I'm prepared for anything,* she told herself. Whatever it is, it will be all right. She closed her eyes tight, then opened them.

And there was her name at the end of the list! She had made it.

Victory, a victory! That night, when she went to bed, not even the slightest thought of Bob or Alison crossed her mind. They had vanished and could not touch the new life that Laurie was about to begin.

Sixteen

Laurie was tempted to shout that she had made the chorus, but though it was on the tip of her tongue and she wanted so much to tell Greg, she remained silent. Mr. Rappaport had made it clear that she would have to learn to read music within a short time. She would learn; one way or another she would read music at the end of two weeks.

She froze with panic after school the following Tuesday when the chorus met. As a cheerleader she knew no fear whatever. She could "sis, boom, bah" and "yeah, rah, rah" as easily as anyone and go through the routines with style and dash. At least the coach and many others had said so. But this was something entirely different.

"All right, everyone, let's begin!" Mr. Rappaport said as everyone milled around the Music Room. "We've got a wonderful program coming up this spring, performances at three different festivals, two statewide contests to enter and, of course, our concert. First sopranos . . ."

As a second soprano, Laurie found herself standing beside a husky blond girl, Bonnie, who talked to the girl on the other side and hardly noticed Laurie. But the girl who was Laurie's other neighbor immediately became friendly.

"Hello, you're new in chorus, aren't you? I'm Kathi Wong."

"Laurie Hudson. This is my first time here."

Kathi blinked her eyes. "Your name is familiar. Don't tell me, I've got to remember for myself how I know your name. . . ."

Laurie laughed to herself. At first it had hurt when so few people knew she was the head cheerleader or remembered that she'd been Homcoming Queen — so much for glory!

And then Kathi did remember. "You were Homecoming Queen and you were so beautiful. I'll never forget."

"That was a long time ago. Tell me about chorus. I'm really scared. Do you have to sing alone and read a lot of music?"

"Don't be scared. Anything can happen. Sure, we read lots of music, but Mr. Rappaport is nice; even when he gets all excited about the music and yells a little, he's still nice. He wants us to be perfect. Today we'll just warm up."

Apparently Mr. Rappaport was every bit the perfectionist Kathi said he would be. "I've got a tape of the Christmas Concert. It went over well, but perfect? No. Basses, you got lost in one place. Sopranos, you were a trifle flat in the motet. We'll all go over the tapes one of these days. Our Spring Concert is going to be *perfect*. Understand?"

He grinned as though he had great surprises in store, but first, he said, they must find their voices. Now Laurie learned a warm-up routine, scales and arpeggios beginning low, going higher, then descending. Everyone sang "What Shall We Do Today?", exaggerating the vowels for emphasis. Mr. Rappaport talked briefly about the importance of breath and of breathing and how it affected awareness.

Why, Laurie thought, *Greg says much the same thing about running.* It seemed curious to her but not improbable, that a connection existed between running and singing.

Mr. Rappaport then asked how everyone would like to do a round, "Sumer Is a Cumin In." Enthusiasm swept over the group and it seemed everyone in the chorus except Laurie knew it. She listened, frantically trying to hear what was going on, but though Mr. Rappaport noticed this, he said nothing. Nor did he say anything when Laurie failed to sight-read the music he handed out. Laurie stared at the notes as though they would make sense if only she concentrated enough.

"Watch me, watch me! Keep your books down!" Mr. Rappaport called out, and she was compelled to watch him. The graceful movements of his arms and the nodding of his head and the slight swaying of his body made the music understandable, but then she lost her place while everyone around her was singing out with all their strength.

How would she ever learn to read music in two weeks when it all seemed so complicated? Mr. Rappaport had them try one piece after another, touching each lightly.

"It's a smorgasbord today — just a taste. On Thursday we'll begin to work," he said.

She had never heard such glorious music, and though she stood in the middle of it while everyone around her sang, it seemed impossible that she would ever keep up. She was not at all surprised when Mr. Rappaport asked her to come to see him after the rehearsal. So this was it, a short-lived choral career for Laurie. But then he asked Kathi to come as well.

"Kathi, do you want a job?" he asked. "Would you like to teach someone to read music in two weeks? Think you can do it?"

"Sure, anything," Kathi answered. She laughed confidently.

"I think we can get some helpful credits for you if you do. Of course, two weeks may take care of the first principles, but it's up to you,

Laurie, to study and to practice. What do you say?"

Laurie and Kathi looked at one another and both may have felt they were being challenged. "Okay," they said simultaneously.

"It's a deal then. Good luck!" Mr. Rappaport said.

"Let's get going now. You have an hour?" Kathi asked. "I don't want to lose any time because he thinks I can't teach you, and I know I can. But you've got to study."

"And if I don't?" Laurie asked, knowing very well nothing could keep her from learning to read music, but Kathi was a bright-eyed person who almost seemed to ask for teasing. She could take it and she could give it — Laurie was enchanted.

"If you don't study, I'll spank you. So watch out!" Kathi said.

The girls found a bench in the courtyard of the school. Kathi took out a sheet of paper and drew the staff, five horizontal lines across the page. "Okay, let's go!" she said.

She taught well, demanding that Laurie answer quickly, and yet it was kind of a game. At the end of the hour Laurie knew she was well on her way to understanding, although it would take practice before she could sight-read.

"It's funny," Kathi said as they walked along the street. "This thing about music. You can't really fake it. You can get away with it once in a while, but if you want to get anywhere, you have to know it."

"Kathi, you're such a great teacher. I'd like to give you something for helping me out. I appreciate it so. What can I do for you?"

Before she could finish, Kathi put her hand to Laurie's arm. "Somebody taught me. I was even more green about it than you. So when you learn to read, you teach someone else."

Oh! But I won't be here next year, Laurie thought, and then snapped her fingers. "There's my little sister. It's time she learned something useful. Of course I'm not sure she'll take anything from me."

"Like my kid sister and my kid brother," Kathi sighed.

They lingered on the street corner, talking even while it grew dark and chilly. Then they had to separate and go to their homes.

So many things were happening in one day. Chorus, music-reading lessons, and now a new friend! Maybe the world hadn't ended after all. Maybe it was just beginning.

The next morning Greg met her as usual, and this time they took a particularly long run out toward the hills. They ran silently, taking on more speed now but still moving easily. Laurie could hardly keep back the news, she wanted so much to tell Greg about the chorus. But since he never talked of himself and most likely would never do so when running, she kept her news to herself.

She would have liked to ask him in for breakfast when they stopped in front of her house, panting after the run, but she feared he would refuse. Yet instead of nodding and running on without stopping, he lingered.

"Congratulations!" he said, beaming.

"What for?"

"Getting into chorus."

"How did you ever know about that? I didn't tell you."

Greg pulled down his expressive eyebrows and whispered confidentially, "The Shadow knows — heh, heh, heh, heh!"

She laughed. "Really, how did you find out?"

"I have spies everywhere."

It was clear he wouldn't answer. "I wish I had spies," she said. "See you later!"

He grinned — oh, those dimples — and then he ran, really ran, so quickly that within minutes he was out of sight. Suddenly she realized she was standing and dreaming, so then she had to rush to shower to get to school on time.

Seventeen

One day Laurie found a neatly written note on her desk in English class. That night she pasted it in her journal.

TRACK MEET. FEBRUARY 7, TWO O'CLOCK. EDGEWOOD HIGH. IN CASE YOU'RE INTERESTED.
                                    GM

It could scarcely be called a love letter, yet Laurie had pressed her lips to it. How different this was from Bob's approach, for he would have ordered her to appear at any game or contest in which he took part! "Honey, you make all the difference in the world. You're my good luck piece. So be there!" Bob's skill lay in sweet-talking her and ordering her around at the same time.

Greg must want her to go to the track meet or he would not have mentioned it. So she wondered why the note had to be so formal and distant, as if the announcement could apply to anyone at all.

A puzzling guy, Greg. If he liked her enough to meet her every morning and run with her at what must seem to him a snail's pace, then why was he so quiet? Why did he never call her by name? Why did he remain so reserved so that even now she knew almost nothing about him?

The next morning when she met him and they ran together, at a faster pace and a greater distance now, Laurie sensed something she could not describe, a kind of glowing over and above all the physical details of running. Never was she more aware of the pounding of her blood, her muscles extending and contracting as she ran and her lungs swelling with every breath, yet the sensation went beyond that, as if she were seeing herself in a new way. *This is me, Laurie. This is what I am. I'm truly alive.*

When they finally slowed down, Greg took her hands in his. She couldn't explain this high, but he understood. "Great, Laurie! I've been waiting for this to happen. You don't have to explain because it's almost impossible to do so. If it happens to you, you understand when it happens to someone else."

"Thanks, Greg. You've been so patient with me. What I don't understand is why you've taken the time to run with me when I know you must be dying to sprint ahead."

Greg pondered over the answer for a moment. "Competition is only one part of running, and it's not necessary for everyone to race. Running is also a way of being alive and finding yourself in a new way. Aren't you learning that?"

"Yes, of course."

"That's only the first step. There's more to come. You'll find out in time."

With that he grinned and left. He had not really answered her question. Possibly he couldn't.

"Well, well, well," Mrs. Hudson said on the morning of the seventh. "You've gone to every competition on the high school campus — football, basketball, swimming, everything but track. And now, you've let everything else go but track."

"So where's there a law saying that I can't change my habits?"

"You're learning," she said.

Though Laurie had gone to more games and contests than she wanted to remember, this was truly different. Fewer spectators waited for the races to begin, but what they lacked in numbers they made up in enthusiasm. Laurie looked for Greg and saw him standing a little apart from everyone else, quiet and calm, yet never more alert. The race was announced.

The contestants lined up and then they were off!

The gentle running she had practiced with Greg each morning could not have prepared her for the forward thrust of speed. Greg's feet hardly touched the ground, his torso was inclined toward the finish line, and when he came in first, his arms raised and his head back, a picture of victory, Laurie could not scream as the other fans did. Excitement and admiration had made her breathless. Greg looked in her direction once, meeting her eyes, and then looked away.

More competitions followed.

Greg, oh, Greg. Now Laurie knew she was in danger of falling in love. What had been at first a mild interest, then a bittersweet pleasure and a constant puzzle, had now become an admiration so fierce and a desire to be held in his arms. Now she knew why the ladies in medieval romances were supposed to swoon when they were in love; the longing was more than they could bear.

However, Laurie, being a twentieth-century American girl at a track meet and not a romantic lady at a twelfth-century joust, had no intention of swooning. She concentrated on the events. Although Greg was not always first, he captured more honors than anyone, and after the meet the reporters and photographers closed in on him, begging interviews and photographs while he stood gracefully, his red headband soaked with perspiration and his shirt clinging to his lean back. A number of girls waited to praise and congratulate him, but Laurie stood back. And then, when he could, he walked over to her.

"So you actually came. I didn't know if you would."

"I wouldn't have stayed away for anything. You were marvelous, Greg."

"Thanks. Not really that marvelous," he said modestly. "This your first track meet?"

"Yes, it's so exciting. I love it."

"Good. Well . . ." He hesitated as though he weren't sure what to say. Then he spoke quickly, ending the conversation. "I'll see you around. Thanks for coming."

Laurie's mind galloped in two directions as she walked home and argued with that common-sense sister of hers. *Laurie, watch it. If you fall in love with Greg, you'll only get hurt all over again.*

Don't be silly. Who's falling in love?

You think I don't know? You've got to be careful. Besides, there are the facts. Don't forget how much he likes that girl, Jean, the one you saw with him when you worked at Pete's. And what about this — he doesn't ever call you or ask you out. He could have asked you out tonight. Instead he says, "See you around." Big deal!

Oh, shut up! Laurie told her far-too-sensible sister. *Anyway, I'm only dreaming and I can keep my thoughts to myself. He'll never know how I feel.*

You're hopeless, Laurie, the practical sister warned.

You bet I am! Laurie cried, and the argument ended for the time being.

$E^{ighteen}$

"Second soprano doesn't sound so great when you sing it alone, but you should hear it with the rest of the chorus. You're all going to have to come to the Spring Concert."

Laurie had just finished practicing the second soprano part in preparation for an upcoming concert. Her parents and Tracy had listened to her as they finished dinner, slightly amazed but pleased. Here was something new.

"Can you actually read all those notes?" Mr. Hudson asked.

"Every single one," Laurie answered. "Actually, I can get the pitch, but I'm a little shaky about the time; it gets intricate with all the grace notes and everything. And it will take practice so I can just toss it off, but that Kathi really gets to me — she's so tiny and so funny and so stern. You don't get away with anything if she's teaching."

"She's a darling," Mrs. Hudson said. "I'm glad you brought her home to dinner the other night. She's welcome any time."

"That's nice, because I've been invited over to her house tomorrow night to meet her family."

Laurie would not admit how rare an occasion it was for her to go out at night, so that even a family dinner at a friend's became an event. Now and then she and Linda got together. Linda was one true friend and Kathi, entirely different, was quickly becoming another. There had never been much time for girl friends when she went with Bob, so this was a new experience.

Though running every morning was the high point of the day, and chorus rehearsals three times a week gave her what she thought was true happiness, she spent evenings alone and the weekends lasted forever. However, sometimes Pete would call and ask if she'd come to the Pizza Palace and work a few shifts.

One afternoon after chorus rehearsal, Kathi spoke to her. "Some of us are going out for Cokes. Want to join us? That will be your reward for singing triplets while the first sopranos sing quarter notes. That's not easy, holding your own like that."

"Nothing to it," Laurie said, "and sure, I'd like to go out with you."

So five of them met at Bowski's Snackerie: Kathi; Lynn Moses, an ethereal blond who sang first soprano; Brenda Pierce, a short, vivacious brunette who claimed she could sing bass if she wanted to; Sue Reuben, a thin girl with a bushel of dark hair. Laurie had been impressed with Sue's sweet and powerful coloratura, which she displayed when she soloed.

Laurie, who had been out only with the girls of the Gang, listened to these girls, who were so very different. They talked freely of anything and everything and laughed freely as well. Someone began to talk about an outside job and then Laurie discovered that all of them worked. They argued about which was better, clerking or waitressing. Kathi announced that Laurie worked at Pete's, and Sue remarked, "Why, that's great. Pete's very particular about whom he hires."

Then it just happened that someone sang a phrase and others joined in — no sooner begun than ended, but Laurie loved the way it happened so spontaneously, the melody enlivening the air as though someone had thrown a rose in their midst.

"Guess who Alex is going with these days?"

The conversation took on a gossipy tinge. "Did you hear about Jennifer and Gary?" "Howard and Dorrie have broken up for good, really!" Laurie sat silently and wondered who these people were. Had they discussed her and Bob and how Alison had broken them up? But that afternoon they never mentioned anyone in the Gang. That could be funny in its way; the Gang considered themselves far above anyone else, and yet these people hardly cared about their existence. So many private worlds in that school, and Laurie wondered where she belonged.

She listened hungrily for a word about Gregory Munson. She wanted to know so much about him, but nothing was said — not a word, not a hint.

They drank Cokes and talked easily until Sue jumped up suddenly and cried, "It's five o'clock! Five o'clock! And I must fly!" It was overdramatic, but Sue could get away with it. There was a quick clatter for change, a brief bit of borrowing here and there, and then they all left Bowski's, scattering like birds who have been feeding together and then fly off at a signal.

Getting together like that happened more and more frequently. Occasionally some of the boys from the chorus joined them and on the springlike days that began to flower, they were content to stand around school and talk lightly.

Laurie began to realize that it was their singing that released them in some way, that in spite of the different backgrounds and the personalities of the group, they seemed to understand each other easily.

Once, when three of the girls from the chorus were dawdling in the park playground on their way home, Greg's name was mentioned. Immediately Laurie noticed her blood flow faster, and she felt as though her ears were standing up as she listened.

"It's Greg's turn to lead the Adventurers. Not this Saturday, a week from Saturday. He doesn't have a track meet, so he can make it," Kathi said.

"What's the Adventurers? I've never heard of it," Laurie said.

"Where have you been?" Kathi and Lynn cried together and then giggled. "It's a kind of outdoor hiking and biking club. It's great."

"And it's also a kind of energy-interest thing."

"But not all the time, because that would be too, too much. Once we visited a windmill farm. Usually we go bicycle riding; sometimes we go for an overnight hike —"

"If we can get two faculty members to go along, too. Once we went to a bird sanctuary near Bolinas. It was fun. What are we doing next?"

"A bike trip. Greg said it wouldn't be strenuous."

"And you believed him? How naive can you get? Greg makes a marathon out of every trip, but of course he's good. I think's he's the best leader. Want to come with us, Laurie?"

"Maybe," she said, careful not to appear too eager. Of course she'd go, nothing would keep her away — not even the one-speed clunker of hers, the one her father had once picked up at a bicycle auction. She'd worry about that when the time came. "I wouldn't mind trying it . . . once."

The following Thursday it rained, a long, tiresome drizzle that dripped everywhere. After chorus the five girls met at Bowski's. After a fit of giggling over some joke, Brenda tapped on her glass with a spoon.

"Announcement, everyone . . . big announcement. Real news! Sue's got a scholarship next year to UCLA."

Genuine surprise and admiration swept through the group. Kathi cried, "When did you find out? How come you didn't let anyone know you were trying out?"

"You're embarrassing me. I had to work awfully hard for it, believe me," Sue explained. "I had to sing and take tests. It wasn't all that easy."

"I should be so lucky," Brenda said.

The conversation now buzzed toward college, scholarships, and other aspirations. It seemed as though everyone planned to go on with school, and everyone was apparently working on scholarships and figuring out ways of getting into one school or another. Brenda would begin at beautician school that summer. Laurie alone had nothing to say.

As she walked home with Kathi, who had invited her for dinner that night, her friend asked, "What are your plans, Laurie? You were very quiet back there."

"I'm not sure anymore," she said.

"You must have thought about it one time or another," Kathi said.

"I did, but I'm not sure about anything anymore," Laurie said, thinking how unquestioningly she had agreed to go to business school so she could learn how to help Bob in his business. Not once had he considered, or had she, for that matter, what she really wanted to do. And now she was certain of only one thing: Business school would be a mistake for her. What else then?

She was easily distracted from this worry by the noisy, enthusiastic welcome she received from Kathi's brothers and sisters. Kathi's grandmother, a tiny, wrinkled woman, made it clear that she, too, welcomed Laurie. The large family sat around the table talking, arguing, laughing . . . all of it lively and so different from the Hudson house.

"No, you can't have silverware!" Mrs. Wong had said the first time Laurie visited. Laurie had to learn to eat with chopsticks, which she used awkwardly at first but now was nearly expert.

"See, it's not hard. Pretty soon you become Chinese," the grandmother said.

"I'd like that," Laurie said, "if I could be like all of you."

She meant it sincerely, for there seemed to be so much confidence in practically everyone there. She wished she had that.

Later when she walked home she realized what had been wrong with her before. She'd had no confidence and therefore had agreed to do whatever Bob wanted her to do. But now she was seeing everything differently. That night she undressed, sat up in bed, and wrote in her journal.

What will I do with my life? I don't have the answer yet, but I didn't even have the question before, which shows how far I had to go. What will I do? What will I become?

The answer *seemed* so simple before. I would be Bob's wife. I would help him in his business while he became rich and well known and all that, which I now think doesn't matter very much. There's no more Bob where I'm concerned, and suddenly I'm beginning to find out there's a *me*.

Maybe not much of *me*, not yet. But I can do three things I didn't know how to do three months ago. I can run, read music, and eat with chopsticks! Ho ho, no career there. But maybe if I learned to do those things, I can learn to do something else that will be part of me, like running and singing.

What? I'd like to go to college, but my grades are poor. I've never studied much. I wonder if I can make up for it.

I wish I could talk with Greg about it. He would say exactly what I needed to know. I'm sure of it. But he's such a puzzle, friendly and yet distant.

I wonder what's going to happen. It's so hard to tell!

That summed it up. She turned out the light and immediately fell asleep but did not dream of college. She saw herself holding hands with Greg while the two of them ran over hills and fields and beaches, like a movie in slow motion.

See, he said, *it's easy when you know how. You don't have to be afraid.*

Nineteen

The comforting mood of the dream was rudely broken the next day when Miss Karlson dropped a bombshell in English class.

"We hear about ecology and conservation and waste and environment so much these days that if you're like I am, you're up to here with it. But that's not a complaint. It's really a good thing, because the messages we hear may be crucial to our well-being or to our very existence. And so, now that it's term paper time, each of you is to choose one aspect of waste and develop your thoughts on the subject."

"Oh, Miss Karlson! You don't *mean* it?"

Groans and applause. Greg would obviously welcome such an assignment, for he had often spoken openly in class and it was clear he was filled with ideas about energy, fuel conservation, and use of resources.

But Laurie worried.

"I don't know what to write," she told her father and mother at dinner. "You hear all this stuff, but I don't want to repeat it. I want it to be good, and I don't know where to begin."

"It's the first time I've ever heard you worry about a school assignment," her mother said.

"Come on, Mom!" Laurie said, although her mother was right. This was the first time she really wanted to do something good. But what?

An idea began to tingle, but she dismissed it as silly, yet ten minutes later it came back in an altered form. Maybe there was something there, but it was out of reach. She went to bed that night, dissatisfied. Maybe she'd have to write about wasting fuel, water, or something of the sort that almost everyone would choose. Something else could be said. She could almost grasp it. Almost. But it eluded her.

The next morning she ran softly and easily as usual but alone, for Greg said he had to get ready for an important track meet and was unable to meet her. The pink fuzz of blossoms lightened some trees; others had just begun to unfurl their new and tender leaves; a magnolia was releasing its large, waxy blossoms and the leaves would come later. It seemed miraculous to Laurie that this should happen year after year, always at the same time.

How was it possible she hadn't really noticed it before as she did now? The question nagged at her. How was it possible that she was experiencing all kinds of new things now, whereas before she had had energy, certainly, and yet . . .

Energy? The word wavered in the air before her. She had had energy, but she had wasted it. Her past life flashed before her: there she was bored at the Gang's many parties, waiting for Bob to take her home; those long, wasted hours when she watched Bob practice when she would rather have been doing something else; all the worry about her clothes and manners because she suspected that Bob's mother had not thought her good enough for her son; all the spent emotion as she pretended she was part of the Gang when actually she never had been. She had known these things for a long time, but now she saw them in a different way — a waste of herself, all her energies, all the power she didn't know she possessed. And perhaps that's why she never really saw the trees coming into bloom and she never really heard music, not in the heightened way she saw and heard it now.

As she ran, her ideas for the essay became clearer. The most valuable energy of all is human energy. Energy of your mind and your body and your senses. Each person must work out his or her understanding of it. It's all too easy to waste it by drifting through the days, being passive, watching television, and not doing anything. But if you listen to your own inner voice, you begin to understand how much power there is within you. It takes work, physical endurance, mental gymnastics, and something more — a determination to *become*. *To become what?*

Here she stopped, not knowing how to finish the sentence, but in time she knew it would come. Putting these thoughts that came rushing toward her into words would not be as easy as she thought, but for the first time in her life she had something to say.

Naturally, she would leave out the personal experiences of her life that led up to this philosophy; she was not about to confess to anyone the events of her life, nor did she have the desire to put down Bob and the Gang. Let them go their way and she would go hers.

When Linda had said, "One day you'll thank Alison for taking Bob away from you," she had thought the remark cruel, for she'd been hurt, but now she saw Linda was right and, thanks to Alison, or fate, or whatever, she was now free to find herself. Now she was discovering who Laurie Hudson was.

"Now, Laurie, you don't have to show us what a diligent student you are by writing at the dinner table," Mrs. Hudson chided her daughter.

"I'm no student, Mom, believe me. It's just that I keep getting ideas for this paper that's due tomorrow, and I have to put them down before I lose them."

She wrote, rewrote, crossed out sentences,

inserted others and saw that her paper, scratched out and written over, was impossible for anyone to read. So she rewrote it neatly and by three in the morning it was finished.

Usually Miss Karlson chose three of the best papers to be read. Greg was invariably asked to read his, and Laurie took it for granted she would never have to stand in front of class to share what she had written. But now, for the first time, Miss Karlson beamed at her and asked her to read her paper.

Laurie panicked. She had led cheers before hundreds of people without blinking an eye, but this was different.

"Would you please read it for me?" she asked Miss Karlson in a timid voice.

"I think you'd better do it. It's yours, Laurie," Miss Karlson said, handing it to her. Laurie saw a big *A* splashed over the first page and a long comment in the margin that she would read later.

Complaints came from the back of the room as she began to read. "Louder, louder!"

"Yes, I think you had a little more volume when you were leading cheers. You could be heard all over the field," Miss Karlson said kindly. Blushing a little, Laurie raised her voice.

Half the class listened and the other half wouldn't have listened to Lincoln giving the Gettysburg Address, but the person she cared about most heard every word; when she was finished Greg Munson made the "A-okay" sign, thumb meeting forefinger, to show his approval.

"Great going!" he said to her as she sat down. Her cheeks burned.

It was not a great victory but a sweet one. The next morning she received an award of sorts.

When she and Greg finished their early morning run, he said, "Want to go on a bicycle hike Saturday?"

"I'll think about it. My bicycle is not exactly young and vigorous."

"If it goes at all, it will be fine. You see, we have this club at school . . ."

"Kathi told me about it. You visit windmills and do all that healthy outdoor stuff."

"I suppose we could do some unhealthy indoor stuff if you prefer," Greg joked. There was that wide grin again, those charming dimples! "This will be a nice little trip. If you want to come, meet us at eight o'clock at the school's west gate, bring a lunch and drinking water. We'll be doing a loop, up to the state park and back."

"Greg, that's a long, long trip."

"I know. But you make the choice. You go or you stay home."

"Thanks a lot," Laurie said uncertainly, not sure she could manage twenty-five or thirty miles on a bicycle.

"What about all that great personal energy you wrote about? Don't you believe what you said?"

"Sure. But twenty-five miles? That's ridiculous."

He grinned again. The dark eyes twinkled. He knew she would come.

"See you Saturday at eight. Don't forget the drinking water!" he said, and then dashed away as lightly as a deer leaping through a forest.

Twenty

"Laurie, what's the matter with you? Robin Hood will never make it that distance," Mr. Hudson said as he hauled out the bicycle from the garage where it had rested—and rusted— for several years now. Its quaint label, ROBIN HOOD, remained bright, but everything else about it had dulled. Even when the spider webs were brushed off and Mr. Hudson had oiled it, blown up the tires, and repaired a few wayward spokes in the wheel, Robin Hood appeared more ready for a quiet old age in a pasture than a long bicycle trip.

"I'm big and strong and I've got energy to spare," Laurie boasted, although the bicycle shattered her confidence more than she would admit.

In the past Bob had let her borrow his bicycles, and they were the newest and the best. But Laurie's borrowing days were finished.

"The bicycle's solid enough," Mr. Hudson said, "but I'm not so sure about you, Laurie. Even with that blue kerchief around your head and all that professional bravado, you're still a girl and not a very big girl either."

"Don't you worry about me, Dad! I've never been stronger. Or later either. *Mom, I've got to leave.* They'll go without me."

"Calm down. I'm almost finished with your lunch."

"But Mom! I can't take all that. Look at it, enough to feed an army!" Laurie counted three sandwiches, half a dozen cookies, apples, carrot sticks, two oranges, a small package of chocolate-covered raisins. She sighed. "Mom, you're supposed to take light, healthy stuff, like beef jerky, dried apricots, granola bars, all that."

"Now listen, young lady, your mother knows a thing or two. You're going to be starving by the time you're ready for lunch — or long before that. So how about a little thanks?"

"Oh, I appreciate it, Mom, and I thank you for fixing the bicycle, Dad, but I don't know how I'm going to *take* all that stuff."

"I'm packing it in your backpack right now," Mrs. Hudson said calmly as Laurie brushed her hair and wondered if she should actually wear the blue kerchief or the red one. But time was passing as she hesitated in front of the mirror.

172

The blue one would be the most flattering, she decided, and then, kissing her father and mother briefly, she adjusted her backpack and left, bicycling as fast as she could so that she wouldn't be late.

Eight bicyclists waited at the west portal in the cool freshness of the morning.

"She's coming. I told you she'd come!" Laurie heard Kathi Wong say. Sometimes Kathi seemed like such a kid it wouldn't have surprised Laurie if she would have jumped up and down when something made her happy. Greg, who was showing some maps to Mark Epstein, the co-leader of the group, acknowledged Laurie's arrival with a hi and a nod of his head. Laurie had hoped he would rush forward, take her hands, peer into her eyes, and say, "I'm so glad you've decided to come, Laurie, so very glad." But he hadn't followed her script.

"Do you know everyone?" Kathi asked, and immediately she began to introduce Laurie to the members of the group, some of whom she had seen before but had never really known.

"This is Ellen Webster. She's one of the founders of the group," Kathi said of the tall, sandy-haired girl who welcomed Laurie with a direct look and pleasant smile. Laurie liked her immediately and wondered if this would be the strong, well-tanned, athletic girl that Greg would admire, or even love.

Mark Epstein looked up from his maps. "Laurie and I know each other. We share two classes. We suffer mutually, right?"

In a way she knew the others in the group. Alex Holden, intense as he fussed with a ten-speed, nodded as Kathi introduced him as the mechanic of the club. Jerry Miller, a self-styled clown, and Alan Gale, a very quiet boy, comprised the rest of male element for that day's outing.

Laurie wondered which of the girls, if any, was the one that Greg liked. Was it Barbara Matthews? Small and cuddly, she was not one Laurie would expect to find in the Adventurers Club. Was it Ellen? How about Kathi? Probably not, since Kathi had once confessed and giggled that she had a boyfriend who lived in San Francisco, Howard Leung. Possibly they were waiting for Jean to show up, although Laurie wondered why she never saw her at school.

What's wrong with me anyway? Laurie scolded herself. If Greg has a girl, it's not really my affair. But the group was growing impatient as they waited for still another person.

"Where's Frankie?"

"Late again, of course. Or has she decided not to show up?"

"It would be just like her. I don't know which is worse, to have her come or have her simply not show up," Barbara said.

"Wait a minute," Greg interrupted. "This

hike is open to anyone who wants to come, and it's going to go better if we all get along."

If Greg spoke severely, his intention was clear and Laurie thought he was justified. Obviously Frankie was less than popular, but Greg felt that everyone should be given a chance to be accepted.

Then again, what if Frankie were the one he liked? Laurie knew her slightly, a frail girl with long, straight, princess blond hair, the only girl who lived on Strawberry Hill who had never been accepted by the Gang. For all her attractiveness, something about her puzzled Laurie and everyone else as well. Yet perhaps because she seemed to belong nowhere, Greg was attracted to her. There she was, worrying again about Greg's personal life when she should be listening to him, for he was talking about the trip.

"Are you all ready to go? It's a demanding trip but it will make you feel virtuous. Besides, the park is worth the trip — it's not a big park, but full of redwoods. We'll picnic there and then start back. Now here are some notes, and most of you know about them already. If a hill is too steep, get off your bicycle and walk. It's no disgrace. The idea is to have a good time, and we don't have to race or speed in order to impress anyone."

"Right," Mark added, "but if you want to drop out for a few minutes, let us know so we don't leave anyone behind."

"Good point," Greg continued. "We have to go along a busy road for a while, can't avoid it, so it's single file as close to the shoulder as you can make it. If the road is really quiet without traffic — and some of those smaller roads will be — we can double up. Change your partners frequently so we all get to know each other. Everybody has water? Anyone need help with your bicycle before we start? Alex will help you. He's a bicycle genius."

Greg had hardly finished when Kathi called out. "She's coming at last. Taking her time, but she's headed this way."

"Hi, Frankie," Greg called out warmly as Frankie joined the group, got off her elegant bicycle, and shook back the long silken locks, which had fallen in front of her face.

"Sorry I'm late. I just can't help it. I'm a Pisces. Greg, what a darling you are to wait for me."

"Everybody's waiting for you," Greg corrected her. If he spoke sharply, Laurie thought he may have done so to cover his true feelings. Frankie's delicacy could be appealing to someone as strong as Greg. Even her voice, faint and thin, was tinged with an accent Laurie couldn't quite identify.

"Before we begin," Greg said cordially, "you do know everyone, don't you? Alex Holden? Laurie Hudson?"

"I know Alex, of course. And Laurie, I know you from somewhere, but I can't quite recall."

Laurie remembered all too well the time Frankie had been invited to one of the Gang's parties. She flirted with all the boys, particularly Bob, and became resentful when he didn't respond. The consensus of the group was that she was one spoiled brat — just as though *they* weren't spoiled — and Frankie was never invited again. Now Frankie "recalled" Laurie with a long drawn-out "Oh."

"Sure, you were the Homecoming Queen and Bob's girl. How is Bobby boy these days? I don't see you with him anymore."

Frankie must have known that she and Bob had separated but chose to be unkind about it, or tactless, or possibly resentful because she had never been invited to join the Gang. Laurie feared that Frankie had no intention of being anything but poisonously sweet toward her. A bad beginning.

"Come on, let's hit the road!"

They began to ride single file. Mark led the group, and Greg offered to bring up the rear during the first part of the ride. He frowned at Laurie's bicycle. "It looks solid. Isn't it a little heavy?"

"I can manage," Laurie said proudly.

"If you need help, holler. Okay?"

Greg's shadow fell on the road as they bicycled west, and she liked knowing that he was there, just behind her. They bicycled through a busy thoroughfare and then turned to a narrower, less-traveled country road. The houses thinned and soon they were passing farms, fields striped with newly planted crops, and pastures on which ewes gamboled with their lambs. Orchards were showing their last pink drift of blossoms and the first flush of green in their leaves. Some of the riders doubled up and talked as they pedaled easily ahead. Frankie made a point of falling behind as she put on a cap to keep her hair out of her face; then she took her place beside Greg, talking with him in a spirited way and possibly amusing him. He said little but occasionally chuckled politely.

Maybe he does like her, Laurie thought with a sinking feeling. Like Alison, Frankie was one of those bold girls who approached boys and flirted openly with them. And it appeared to work. But Laurie could not do that. Possibly she was the one who was spoiled, expecting boys to come to her instead of chasing them.

Whatever thoughts she had were soon diverted as Kathi turned and asked how Robin Hood was doing, and when Laurie said everything was all right, Kathi began to sing, one of the lighter folk songs Laurie had learned in chorus. Laurie sang along with her. And then Alan, who was also in chorus, came up with a hiking song, lively and spirited, and now half the group was singing and harmonizing, loudly through the first two verses and falling off rather badly through the third, when they could no longer remember the words.

"What we oughta do is put on a concert, make some money for the club," Alan said.

"No way," Ellen said. "We want to keep ourselves pure."

"Untainted by filthy money?"

"I'd rather be tainted with that than anything else!" Kathi cried.

"It's not the money. It's just that we're not bright enough to remember the words," Ellen said, and Alan punched her lightly.

The conversation continued easily, here and there with light joking, occasionally punctuated by bits of singing, but as the hill became steeper, Laurie had to concentrate on pushing the pedals. Robin Hood made it over the first hill and slowly exerted itself to get over the second, but when the third hill arose in front of them, Robin Hood balked.

"Come on, come on. You're embarrassing me," Laurie said softly to it as though it were her horse, but it refused to start. Then Laurie noticed that Greg was watching her and a smile played around his lips. He had heard what she said.

"If it were a donkey you could hold a carrot in front of it, but it doesn't work with a bicycle."

"I know. Isn't that a shame! Greg, I hate to be the one who holds everybody else back by walking up the hill."

"Then I'll walk with you, so there'll be two of us. You take half the guilt and I'll take the other half."

"Thanks, Greg, but if you'd rather ride ahead, really I wouldn't mind."

"I wouldn't think of it. Besides, this way we can talk together instead of huffing and puffing."

The others rode on ahead on their slender ten-speeds while Laurie and Greg walked. Unlike their silent morning runs, conversation seemed to be in order.

"I love getting out," Laurie said. "Sometimes I feel as though Edgewood were an island. I haven't been out of it for nearly five months."

"How do you stand it? Not that Edgewood isn't the whole universe rolled up into one nest of suburbia, but there is another world outside."

"For you, Greg, I think that's true. I've never been anywhere else but Edgewood."

"Which doesn't mean you're doomed to stay there forever. You need to get a wider view of everything. And that means getting out. At least I think so. Don't you feel that you would love it?"

"I've just begun to think about it. It's a little scary. I'm not sure."

"That paper you wrote on human energy astounded me, you know, because it mirrors exactly what I think about energy. It begins at home, within yourself. One point you didn't mention that I think about a lot is the ability to develop your wings and spread them so you can fly away. Being free, for one thing, and getting a look at the world, for another. Staying stuck in Edgewood isn't right for you, Laurie."

She felt obliged to defend her family. "We're not exactly glued here. We go to state parks and the beaches. We camp when my father gets a vacation. So I've been around a little, just around here. But riding in a car is nothing like this, getting out and bicycling, or should I say *walking*. You see everything in a different way. I've never really done it before."

"You amaze me, Laurie. Three surprises so far."

"Three? I can't imagine . . ."

"You shock me, lady. First, when I saw you running I was ready to give you the nonathlete's award of the year. Not really — you were in top form as a cheerleader, energetic, spirited and all that. But as a runner? At six o'clock every morning? That threw me."

"I wouldn't have, but my father bought me the outfit, and I couldn't disappoint him. So that explains the running."

"Of course. But you're coming along so well. That's really what amazes me. A very promising pupil."

"Thank you, sir. What's the second surprise?"

"That paper you wrote. I wouldn't have approached the subject exactly as you did, but philosophically we aren't so far apart. My approach is that you are *allowed* so much energy according to your personal strength and by virtue of twenty-four hours a day. What are you going to do with it? Begin to think like that, and it can change your life."

"I like the way you put it."

"Where did you get your idea for your article?"

"One morning when I was running, my thoughts wandered. It worried me that I didn't know what to write. And then, it just came, just like that!"

"While you were running? It figures. Most people think running is a physical thing, putting down one foot after another in a certain way; but there's more to it than that. Only you can't tell a person — he has to experience it for himself."

"Hey, who picked this hill anyway?" someone called out. By this time more than half the adventurers were walking, leading their bikes uphill, but a few diehards were still pumping away.

"What about the third surprise?" Laurie asked. Greg seemed friendly now, very approachable. In a way it was their first conversation.

"That happened this morning when I heard you singing with Kathi."

"Greg, that's not really singing. I've only just learned to read music."

"I wouldn't know about that. You sounded fine. What impressed me was a feeling of spontaneity. Both you and Kathi simply sang, for the love of it, I guess."

"Since we weren't being paid, I guess you could see it that way." Laurie laughed, so pleased that Greg had noticed.

The conversation was interrupted as Frankie approached Greg. "I thought we were supposed to change partners, so we all get around, like you said."

Why, oh why, did she sound as though she were ordering people around? Why was her voice so petulant? Then she changed, becoming kittenish.

"Greg, I think the chain has slipped or something. You'd think that a bike that cost as much as this would run perfectly."

"Not really," Greg said as he stopped to examine it while Laurie held his bicycle. "The finer an instrument is tuned, the more apt it is to have problems. A workhorse like Laurie's will last forever."

"Then I promise not to shoot it or put it out to pasture," Laurie joked, "unless, of course, one of those finely tuned Peugeots comes my way."

In fact, it was already occurring to Laurie that if Pete would give her a job during the summer, she'd buy herself a new bicycle. She watched Greg fix Frankie's bicycle deftly and then all three trudged up the hill. Frankie was taking over, looking up into Greg's face with that curious pixie smile of hers that may have enchanted him, but Laurie didn't stay to find out. Hurrying a little she moved up and walked beside Jerry.

"So you're making it up the hill. Good for you, Laurie. Not everyone makes it the first try."

"Well, I'm just back from a climb up Everest, so this isn't all that bad," Laurie joked, feeling happy and lighthearted. She would not let Frankie spoil this magnificent day when the world seemed ready to spring forth with new growth everywhere. Nor could she, or Jerry either, say much as they puffed up this extraordinarily steep hill.

At last they reached the top, and on the other side the vista caught her breath. Fields, hills, fences, a dark patch of pines, and a row of Italian cypresses piercing the skies lay spread out below. A freshly plowed field gave off the odor of rich, moist soil, and gulls fluttered and wheeled after a tractor that turned over the deep brown earth. Above, skies of the purest blue allowed a flock of white clouds to move gently in the wind.

"Oh, word, I cannot hold thee close enough . . ."

This line from the Edna St. Vincent Millay poem coursed through Laurie's mind and then she saw that Greg, standing beside her, caught her glance. Was it possible they were thinking the same thing?

For a moment everyone stood at the top of the hill, recovering from the climb. And then, suddenly, Greg mounted his bicycle.

"Geronimo!" he cried, and sailed down the hill, surely as steep on the descent as on the climb. One by one the other cyclists followed. Laurie was frightened, really frightened, but there was no such thing as walking downhill, so she prayed a little, got on her bicycle, and *went*! The wind rushed against her, pushed back her hair, flattened her jacket against her, and whistled past her ears as Robin Hood descended faster and faster, actually taking her halfway up the next hill.

She rode until she could not push the bicycle anymore. Then she got off and walked to the top of the next hill, laughing out loud. She could not remember having enjoyed anything more.

After one brief stop during which everyone drank water and Kathi passed around licorice sticks, they continued the ride, less hilly now, and reached the state park about two o'clock. They parked their bicycles and collapsed under the redwoods.

"Tired?" Kathi asked.

"I don't mind a rest," Laurie said modestly, though she had never looked forward to one more than at that very moment. "What about you?"

"I never get tired," Kathi boasted lightly, winking at Laurie to show this was not quite true.

"Some guys have all the luck," Ellen Webster said with mock envy, but she was the one who could probably have bicycled forever. She sat down, not collapsing like the rest of the group, but unwinding as she massaged her legs.

Laurie sank down gratefully along with everyone else and, lying on the soft damp forest floor, peered up at the giant trees and the radial spokes that emanated from the massive trunks. It was quiet here, quiet as a cathedral. Then Mark broke the silence.

"Hey, aren't we ever gonna have lunch?"

"I thought you'd never ask!" Immediately a clamor of voices and a renewal of energy changed the mood as Kathi set out a red-and-white checked cloth that had been hidden in her pack. Everyone piled their contributions on this, something Laurie had not expected. Kathi contributed tiny tinfoil packages, which turned out to be chicken wings cooked Chinese style. Ellen had managed to keep a salad of lettuce and vegetables in her backpack. A few packages of cheese. Cold meats. Fig Newtons. Laurie cut the sandwiches her mother gave her into quarters and although she hardly thought they represented the last word in fine cuisine, they disappeared quickly. Frankie produced an expensive, rich chocolate fudge cake and, though only two forks were available, it disappeared within seconds. Everyone lay around, contented and lazy.

Then Frankie attacked Laurie. It was such a surprise that Laurie could not believe she heard the high, thin voice. "We're all friends here, Laurie, so why don't you solve the mystery for us and tell us what happened to you and Bob?"

"Hey, Frankie, cool it!" someone said. Others murmured some protests.

That anyone could speak so bluntly and crudely, particularly a stranger, left Laurie open-mouthed. Not wanting to make an issue over it, she got up and walked over to the cabin marked WOMEN. Kathi and Ellen followed immediately. A hush fell over the group, and then one of the boys asked what route they would be taking home, obviously trying to change the subject.

"Someone ought to gag that Frankie forever," Kathi said. "I'd do it but it's against the rules."

"Don't mind what she says," Ellen explained. "She likes to dig into everyone. That's how she is. A hopeless case."

"But what is she doing in a club like this? She's the only one who seems really out of it, as if she doesn't belong. I know I'm here for the first time and I shouldn't say this . . ." Laurie trailed off.

"But you happen to be right. She's a pill and we can't kick her out."

"Can't someone say something?"

"Greg is aware of it, but he says that going for hikes and the natural surroundings should mellow her. He believes that's one of the functions of the club. She stays. He won't stand for snobbery of any kind," Ellen explained.

"But why did she attack me? What have I done to her?"

"Laurie, you are naive, aren't you?" Kathi said. "She used to be in love with Bob but you were there; then Alison came along and she never got in edgewise. And now she's after Greg, and she can't stand to see him talking with you, or with anyone else, so that explains it."

"Do you think that Greg really likes her?" Laurie asked.

Kathi and Ellen appeared to consult each other. "You can't tell with Greg."

"She's appealing in her way. But Greg is quiet about his personal life."

"Does he take her out at all?" Laurie asked as casually as she could, but Kathi and Ellen burst out laughing.

"So Greg's gotten to you, too! You do care what he thinks." Ellen laughed. "Like everybody else."

Laurie flushed. "Of course not. He's a good leader and a good runner, but as far as anything else is concerned, why . . . why . . ." she practically stammered, not knowing what to say.

"You can't fool me," Kathi cried, as devilishly as a kid sister. "You like Greg."

"Kathi!" Laurie tore the peel from the orange she had been eating and pretended to wash Kathi's face with it while she doubled over with laughter.

"Since you're new, I'll tell you a secret, in

case you hadn't guessed," Ellen said. "It's a club rule. You have to fall in love with Greg."

"Oh," Laurie said, keeping cool. "Are you in love with him, Ellen?"

She nodded, grinning widely.

"Me, too, me, too," Kathi said, laughing until she had to hold her sides.

They were making fun of her, but so gently that she poured water on her hands and flicked it toward them all, which helped take away the sting of Frankie's remark.

"Hey, are you guys going to stay in there forever or are you taking a trail hike with us?" someone called.

With that the girls emerged into the clear cool air and walked with the others along the paths under the redwood trees. When they were back from the hike, Greg called everyone together.

"We'd better get started. We have more than half the way to go but we aren't retracing our steps and the hills aren't very steep. Yet there could be traffic, so everyone ride carefully. Okay?"

"Oh, Greg," someone said, "you sound like a grandfather with all that advice."

"If you want to get splattered all over the road, do it on your own time, not on ours. Five minutes. And then we're leaving."

Since Laurie was ready to leave, she stretched out under the trees and let her eyes follow the vertical thrust of the trunks that pushed up into the sky. Peaceful now, she closed her eyes, but opened them when something soft with a sweet, woodsy scent brushed across her face. Greg was sitting beside her, tickling her face gently with the soft, needled tip of a small redwood branch.

"Do you like it here, Laurie?"

"There aren't words to describe it. And you?"

"You can practically grow stronger just by being under these fine old giants. Stronger and more serene."

Laurie was thinking less about strength and serenity and more about how she wished Greg would take her in his arms right there on the bed of dried needles. The desire came with such force that it nearly frightened her. Did he understand? Was it possible he felt the same attraction or was he thinking about the energy of the trees? Or of Frankie? Or Jean or some other girl?

"Hey, you guys. Your five minutes were up ten minutes ago," Mark cried. "Are we going or aren't we?"

"Sure. What's your hurry?" Greg said, springing up.

The hikers moved to where they had parked their bicycles and as Laurie was adjusting her bike bag, she was suddenly aware that Frankie was staring at her with a resentment and bitterness so dreadful, that again she was shocked. The next minute Frankie was turning up her pretty face toward Greg and she made some funny remark, for he laughed. She could be amusing, tantalizing. What if Greg liked that lightness, since he himself was so serious?

Laurie felt grateful when at last Mark cried impatiently, "Let's *go!*" And then they all started for home.

The ride home was easier; that is, less hilly and less attractive than the route out to the park. Although Frankie made a point of riding as close to Greg as possible, Alex Holden seemed to have developed an interest in Laurie and rode his bicycle beside her as much as he could.

"Let's stop for a cold drink. I'm dyin' of thirst," Frankie said.

"Not a bad idea!" Since everyone agreed, they all piled into Herbie's, a small roadside snack bar, and Greg made a point of sitting beside Laurie. Once or twice he seemed on the verge of saying something, but stopped. His remarks, whatever they might have been, hung unfinished in the air.

"Five o'clock and let's go!" Mark cried. "I've got a date tonight. Did you hear me, Greggy dear?"

"Sure, I heard you. Okay, back to the road."

Laurie didn't know whether her imagination had become oversensitive or whether Frankie had been watching her and Greg, but at any rate her attitude had changed. She had become silent, but it was ominous, worse than her chatter. For Laurie she was the one dark cloud in a day filled with radiance. But Laurie didn't think about her, for she couldn't remember ever being more exhausted and she still had five miles to bicycle.

As they pedaled single file at the edge of a road, which was becoming increasingly busy with traffic, Laurie wondered if she had ever been happier, and nothing came to mind. Being crowned Homecoming Queen had seemed the most glorious thing that had happened to her at the time, but in retrospect it was relatively unimportant; the dance that followed and her evening with Bob were as dull as anything she could imagine. For the first time she could confess to herself that this was so. But on this day, being with people she genuinely liked, being with Greg, and getting out to new and beautiful areas, made her want to sing.

Her reveries ended as a scream pierced the air, followed by a screech of brakes and a loud clamor of horns. Frankie had turned her bike toward the road and barely escaped being run over. In a flash of truth, Laurie caught the intensity in Frankie's eyes as she stared ahead and with a shock, Laurie knew that Frankie had staged the scare and was now out of control.

So much happened in less than two seconds. Miraculously Greg burst forward and grabbed Frankie's bicycle, pulling her out of the way. The driver of the car yelled something obscene, and other drivers stared at the group belligerently as the traffic started to flow again.

Had Greg exploded at Frankie, nobody would have blamed him, for he had risked his life to save her. As leader of the group he felt his responsibility keenly. Yet, although everyone else in the group was shocked and furious at Frankie, Greg put his arm around her and held her. "It's all right," he said in a low, comforting voice as if she were a hurt child, for she was obviously shaken by the experience. Her body shook nervously and her lips chattered.

Suddenly Laurie felt ashamed of herself for having been so critical of Frankie. But it was only natural for someone in the group to voice a complaint, for Frankie had jeopardized them all. Alan began to say something, but Greg put his finger to his lips, meaning they should all wait silently.

"Would you like some water?" Kathi asked, offering her bottle.

"Thanks," Frankie whispered in a voice so subdued, a little girl's voice, that Laurie hardly recognized it. She was a strange and complex creature, this Frankie.

Mark led the group, Frankie rode next to the end, and Greg brought up the rear so that he could watch what was happening. As they approached their homes in Edgewood, individuals waved good-bye and pedaled off.

"Greg," Frankie said in her little-girl voice. "It was grim, having such a close call, and I'm still shaking. Would you ride home with me? Please?"

Pretty please with lots of sugar on it! That's how Laurie would have described the voice. Everyone waited for Greg's reply. He chose a reply that could not have been reassuring to Frankie.

"Since I'm group leader for today, I guess it's my responsibility."

Frankie lived farther away than anyone else. The five people left in the group peeled off one by one and then there were three. Although Laurie's house was slightly out of the way, Greg insisted on seeing her home.

"Thanks for the wonderful time. It was almost perfect," she said as she got off her bicycle.

"I'm glad you came. Please come again," Greg said.

And then he rode off with Frankie as he had promised. And Laurie went into her house, exhausted and happy — and puzzled. It had been an *almost* perfect day.

Twenty·one

Never had Laurie's days been so full. She never consciously used the words *happy, lucky,* or even *unlucky* as she thought of her present life. She was too busy to dwell on such concepts.

The spring term was flying by. Laurie had appeared with much nervousness and high excitement in several concerts given by the chorus, and the Spring Concert was yet to come. She now read music fairly easily. Though she knew only what she sang in chorus, she found herself hungry to learn more and more songs.

"I don't think there could be such a thing as too much music," she said to Kathi.

"I feel that way, too," Kathi answered, "and

since we'll both be going to Community College in the fall, let's try out for glee club or choir. Okay? If you really want to sing, you can always find a choir or some group that will want you."

"I hope so. I never dreamed I would love it so much."

She could not understand exactly why music should satisfy her so deeply. Oddly enough, running could do that, too. Although on the surface running and singing seemed to have little in common, both were concerned with breathing and both could give Laurie feelings of being high, practically floating.

"Do you get a sense of being high when you run?" she asked Greg one morning.

"Sure, especially in races. You know the Greek statue of Hermes with wings on his feet? Sometimes that's how I feel, as if I'm flying over the ground and not touching it. But don't tell anyone I said so. They wouldn't understand."

"Okay, Hermes, I won't." Laurie laughed. "I understand what you mean."

She and Greg ran silently, seldom talking, although they might exchange a few words afterward. From time to time he made practical comments. Her form was improving, and she could begin to think about taking longer runs. Or he would suggest a kind of sock she might find more comfortable. Sometimes they ran a new route, through parts of Edgewood she had not seen before even though she'd lived there for such a long time. Even those streets she had seen before now appeared to be in a different light.

She wanted very much to ask him questions, for she was nearly out of her mind with curiosity. Where did he live? What was his family like? Who was Jean? What did he want to do with his life? Was he attracted to Frankie and did he mind the rumors spreading around the school that she would go to the Senior Prom with him?

But she could never ask such personal questions. Nor did he ever ask her anything more personal than questions about running or her opinions on wildlife preservation and population control. Her answers to his questions were sketchy, but she liked listening to him as he discussed them.

In a way, Laurie thought, not knowing such things as his father's occupation, what his mother's work was, or how many brothers and sisters he had gave their relationship a kind of purity.

He encouraged her to go on outings with the Adventurers, and she agreed. In early May there would be an overnight trip to Point Reyes. "What, you've never been there?" he asked, shocked. "Then you *are* going!"

Very often when he left her in the mornings he looked at her as though he were about to say something important, but he never did. Once he took both her hands in his and squeezed them tight, and then he had run on.

How strange it was that though Bob had kissed her often and sensually, never did it give her the excitement that the touch of Greg's hands did.

But did he like her really? And if so, when would he tell her? When?

Twenty-two

The Adventurers Club trip to Point Reyes was drawing near.

"You've got to come, Laurie," Greg said. "I can't believe you've never seen it. There's so much there — the cliffs, the beaches, the seals, the birds; this time of year there'll be flowers. In winter, you can watch the whales. You've got to come."

"I know, but then you don't know my parents. An overnight hike? There'll be a struggle about that."

"But two members of the faculty will be going with us. Miss Karlson, would you believe? And Mr. Andrews, the P.E. teacher. Do you know him? It's perfectly okay. We'll go there in the schoolbus because otherwise it's too far. But we'll bike through Marin County for fifteen miles or so to Bear Valley, the park headquarters. Then we'll hike. I guess you don't have to tell your parents we'll be crossing the San Andreas fault . . . and then we'll set up camp at one of the campgrounds. Laurie, Laurie, you must come."

She wanted nothing more than to do just that. "I will. It will mean a battle at home, but I'll come anyway. You'll see!"

"No, absolutely no. The day hikes are scary enough, but an overnight hike with all the stuff that goes on with young people today. Not for my daughter."

"Oh, Dad, it's not what you think. Anyway, there will be two faculty members there."

"Can't trust them either," Mr. Hudson said. "When I was growing up, we didn't do things like this. Leads to trouble."

Laurie appealed to her mother, who said lightly, "I'll think about it. And Bill, if you don't get out of this house now, you're going to be late for work."

"Don't you two plan anything behind my back," he said as he left.

"When your father gets a stubborn streak, don't say anything. Don't make waves. He'll only get worse. He has to get used to the idea. But I'm not so sure I like it myself."

"Mom, I thought you were on my side."

"You're changing, you know."

"This group is a hundred times safer and better than the Gang."

"But things can happen even so."

"The way you say *things* it's as if you were some Victorian. I've got my own ideas and my own ethics, don't you know that? Anyway, there's no love in my life. Not in the least."

"And who is this Greg who meets you every morning when you're running, this Greg who's the head of the Adventurers Club, the one who had a fiery letter in the Edgewood Journal about the need for more street trees here, and protested cutting down those in Ogden Grove so they can put up a shopping center. He's just a casual friend, I suppose."

"Could be," Laurie said, hoping her face would reveal nothing. "No indications of anything else."

"I've an idea he helped you get over Bob."

"Bob who?" Laurie asked, and then laughed. "Oh, Mom, I'm so lucky! If that sneaky Alison hadn't come along, I might still be with him. A fate worse than . . . I don't even want to think about it."

"You're mending nicely," Mrs. Hudson said. But Laurie, unwilling to pursue that subject in light of more important issues, touched her mother's arm. "Please, Mom, I want to go on this hike more than I've ever wanted anything. Please talk with Dad. Let him see I'm not just some silly thing who'll go crazy with freedom. I know what I'm doing. I'm grown up now, more than I ever was before."

Mrs. Hudson became serious. "I believe you, Laurie. At one time I wouldn't, but now I do.

Okay, I'll see what I can do about your father."

"Thanks, Mom. You're a doll."

"One thing more. If we said no, would you manage to go anyway?"

Laurie was about to answer, but grinned instead. "Why don't you just say yes and let me go along and have a good time? That way you'll never have to find out what I'd do."

"Maybe you ought to go to law school," Mrs. Hudson said. "You put out a highly convincing case. And now, off to school with you or you'll be late."

At seven in the morning, on a particularly sunny spring day, fourteen members of the Adventurers Club met at the school. Unfortunately, Frankie appeared among them, with the fanciest camping gear Laurie had ever seen. Frankie had not caused any more dramatic upsets on the hikes taken after Laurie's first bicycle hike, but she clung to Greg when she could. And if Greg allowed it, it was his affair, not Laurie's.

Nothing could ruin the weekend. Nothing at all. Seat-changing was the rule of the ride and since everyone did it, there was never any need to feel hurt or left out. All one had to do was tap someone else on the shoulder and exchange seats. This way everyone became better acquainted.

First they had to pass the Bay Bridge that led to San Francisco. The city gleamed white and sparkling, miraculously free of smog. The bus did not linger there but drove through to the Golden Gate Bridge. It was during this part of the ride that Greg had made his way to the seat beside Laurie. However, three times before others had tapped his shoulder and he had had to move on, but he always came back. This was already the butt of several jokes and comments, but Laurie was grateful that nobody interrupted as they crossed the Golden Gate Bridge.

"It's a magnificent structure, isn't it? Lots of people compare it to a cathedral. It has that feeling, doesn't it?" he said.

His hand brushed hers as they passed under the high red-orange towers that rose into the purest of blue skies. Below them the waters gleamed. Since knowing Greg, it seemed that the whole world took on a beauty she had not noticed before.

But she had been here before, one time when Bob's family was taking her out to dinner in the hilly, picturesque town of Sausalito. It must have been beautiful then, but she did not remember its beauty, only that Bob's parents had quarreled all the way and then had sat in strained silence during the meal. Again she realized how lucky she was to be free of that family forever.

"Actually, I've been here before," Laurie told Greg, "but I like to think I'm seeing it for the first time with you."

Then she turned to the window, her face suddenly red. One does not say things like that. She feared he would think she was another Frankie, falling in love, hanging all over him.

But he could not reply to Laurie at all because Jerry Miller tapped him on the shoulder, and he had to leave while Jerry, cracking jokes wildly, sat down beside Laurie.

The bus traveled up the highway and eventually stopped at their departure point. The bicycles were taken down from the top of the bus and the packs thrown out. Eventually everyone got their backpacks and bicycles and pedaled off through rolling hills, occasional groves of eucalyptus, and pastures. The narrow road curved gently, and except for the sounds of their voices and an occasional laugh, Laurie felt the quiet of the country, broken only by the insistent crow of a rooster, the clucking of hens, or the lowing of a head of dairy cows. Long before they could see the ocean, Laurie was aware of it, a tremendous force vibrating and waiting there, behind the hills, beyond the road.

Soon they reached the visitors' center, a small building beside a huge red barn. They left their bicycles there and began to hike down a country road, more a wide path than anything else, with trees on either side and all kinds of woodland blooms. Now and then well-groomed horses, straddled by straight-backed riders, crossed the path. The breeze blew mildly, welcoming the travelers.

"But remember," Mr. Andrews said, "when you cross the ridge to the ocean side, we might find a chilling fog and strong winds. The weather changes here from hour to hour. So watch it!"

The warning appeared ridiculous at the moment. Laurie could imagine nothing more than this perfection of weather, this ideal spring morning. Kathi began to sing and soon everyone, whether born singer or not, joined in. Nor did it matter that half of the group didn't know the songs but sang along anyway. They sang every combination of song: an old English round, then a spiritual that had been sung in chorus. Then Jerry Miller, in the most purposely obnoxious voice he could find, sang commercials, one after the other until someone pretended to gag him with a kerchief. Frankie complained of a stone in her shoe so everyone waited while she emptied it and then went on. Quiet Alan Gale came out with a Bogey imitation, and then to everyone's surprise, Paul Roderick began to sing some country and western songs in a hauntingly sweet voice. It was Ellen Webster who was able to join him.

Greg walked beside Laurie and grinned at her from time to time, stopping as he heard noises in the bushes to point out small birds hovering over a nest. He would have to identify them later. Laurie was less interested in the names of the birds than in Greg's intensity. He seemed to take in everything, as if he, too, were part of nature rather than, like most of the others, simply someone who came to dip into it for a while.

The road was dappled with shade and sun as everyone hiked along. Greg and Laurie stopped, watching breathlessly the flash of blue as two jays flew across the road. Soon the roar of the ocean could be heard, low and rumbling.

I am perfectly content now, she thought to herself; there was nothing more that she wanted than to be walking beside Greg on this golden green morning with the turquoise sky above and the salty fragrance in the air. They climbed a rise of hill where fine sand shifted around tufts of shining, swordlike dune grass.

"Be careful," Mr. Andrews shouted. "That stuff can cut you."

Immediately four people experimented, running their fingers up the grass to see if it would actually cut them. But Greg and Laurie moved toward one side and stood on the hill. The Pacific was spread out before them, gleaming blue and green and sparkling with thousands of diamond points as the sun hit the crest of the waves. The waves rose, then crashed into a roar of churning foam that subsided as the waves reached the beach, which was then pulled back as though the ocean were ordering it to return. A dozen sandpipers ran along the edge of the wave, pecking here and there for whatever morsel they could find, playing just ahead of each wave, scurrying on legs as slender as the finest twigs.

"This is so beautiful," Laurie said in a voice so low that only Greg could hear her, "that if this were my last day on earth, I'd be happy."

"Don't talk like that. Not ever. Nothing about dying or last days on earth," Greg said with a vehemence she had never heard in him. Her words had upset him, something she would not have believed possible.

"What's the matter, Greg? It was only a way of talking. I have every intention of living. Come on, you mustn't take it so literally."

"You must be careful about saying things like that," he said, quieter now, and then he was himself once more. "Hey, I think everyone's having lunch. Come on. Aren't you hungry?"

They separated and they sat with others, not wanting to appear too standoffish, but Laurie wondered why Greg had spoken so severely. At this point he was laughing and chatting, joking with everyone, for he was capable of being highly sociable when he chose. Everyone ate as if they were famished, and afterward they lay back lazily and watched the terns wheeling above and the cormorants skimming over the water. Now and then they could hear the sea lions barking.

It's so good to be with people you really like, Laurie was thinking as her eyes traveled over the group. However, she found it hard to like Frankie, who was edging up close to Greg and insisted on feeding him a giant chocolate chip cookie. Greg laughed politely but seemed a little annoyed. Laurie frowned, unable to understand why Greg put up with her silliness unless — oh, no, unless he really *liked* her? It made no sense.

"Okay, everyone, we'd better get to camp," Alan called. Though he was quiet, he showed he could lead the group, and so reluctantly everyone got up, hoisted up their backpacks and sleeping bags and trudged along the trail that led to the Wildcat Campground, a pleasant, open place in a grassy meadow near a stream. It was necessary to put the food on shelves well off the ground so that the raccoons and foxes couldn't get to it.

After everything was settled, they were free to hike along the beaches. Cliffs towered above them and they were warned they could crumble easily, so the group stayed away. They were also warned not to go swimming. Although it was relatively safe on that portion of the beach, the undertow was particularly vicious that day.

"It's a good thing we brought our jackets with us," Kathi said, and Laurie agreed. Gone was the gentle, springlike wind and the clear blue skies. Sheets of fog began to drift, and the colors changed from the brilliant blues and greens of the water to sullen, grayed blues and murky depths. Laurie shivered a little as the wind blew, and yet the excitement of being there had not dimmed.

They seemed to walk forever. "At this rate we'll be in Oregon tomorrow!" Jerry quipped. And yet Laurie found it all so incredible. The beaches seemed to extend forever. Up ahead were rocks rising from the water where waves crashed against them, sending out a spray. So many contradictions in a way — the serenity of space, with the ocean stretching out forever, interrupted by the violence of the waves that seemed to be growing more and more fierce as the afternoon wore on. Yet California poppies survived, clinging here and there to the dunes. Laurie and several others kneeled to examine a tide pool, and Greg squatted beside her.

"That's a starfish and, oh, look at the tiny crabs!" Laurie said, quite excited over the discovery while someone else named all the forms of life in the tide pool.

Frankie edged in between Laurie and Greg. "You two are always telling secrets. That's not very friendly. I thought this was supposed to be the kind of club where everyone is open and sociable and democratic. Getting off by yourselves isn't exactly that."

"Actually, Frankie, that was never written into the bylaws, although I'm not sure that we have bylaws. You can't regulate things like that. But I guess we should be sociable, so I'll whisper one of our secrets right in your ear, just so you won't feel left out."

If Laurie was exasperated with Frankie, she saw the glint of humor in Greg's eyes as he whispered, loud enough for Laurie to hear, "Sea anemones aren't flowers; they're *animals*!"

"That's just great," Frankie said sarcastically, then she left Greg and went over to unsuspecting Alan and slipped her arm through his, which embarrassed him painfully.

"Now there's a difficult woman," Greg said of Frankie. "However, she has a point. We should be part of the group when we're out camping like this. It's not my choice at the moment."

"Nor mine, either," Laurie said. "I like seeing everything with you."

Reluctantly they separated and mingled with the others in the group. Mark wanted to hike down the beach to a place where geological formations had turned the earth into a kind of sculptural gallery with tunnels, caves, stacks, and tide pools.

Laurie was not the only one to find herself shivering in the growing onslaught of winds. The sky had turned a menacing steel gray and the ocean took on a pewter cast, tipped with frothy white caps.

"I can't believe the weather can change so fast," Kathi said.

"Listen, everyone," Mr. Andrews said. "Warning, warning. It's later than you may realize. And the tide will be coming in soon, so everyone, watch out! Let's keep together."

Everyone agreed as they walked along the beach, but when they reached Sculptured Beach, the warning was forgotten as everyone explored the region individually, climbing through the natural tunnels, scrambling over the rocks, and studying the caves. Laurie climbed over some upended rocks with Ellen and Alex and all three found a large tidal pool surrounded by algae-covered rocks.

"Look at it!" Ellen cried. "I've never seen one so large."

"Or so gorgeous," Alex said. "Look at the starfish, wow!"

Thoroughly entranced, Laurie kneeled near this miniature world in which tiny schools of transparent fish swam confidently past flower-like anemones. Tiny crabs scuttled sideways. Periwinkle shells of transparent blues and purples gleamed through the clear water, and green sea plants waved gently in the water. Laurie put her hand in the water and drew out several small pink shells, and she found it amazing that at one time soft, minuscule sea animals had lived in them.

The world is so full of a number of things. She wished Greg were with her so they could explore this together, but he was off somewhere with the others. Maybe someday they would get diving suits and explore the bottom of the ocean.

How great it is to be alive, she thought, *with so much to see, to do, to become part of!* Just by observing this tidal pool, she felt, in some way she could not explain, part of its history.

Lost in her thoughts as she watched a crab laboriously climbing over a stone, which must

have seemed like a boulder to him, she did not
realize that Ellen and Alex had left to join the
others, nor did she realize until a wave broke
over her leg that the tide must be coming in.

She could see the group moving away from
the water; most of them were farther inland,
examining what looked like a tunnel. Thinking she had better join them, she got up; slipping over the wet algae, she caught her foot
in the small crevice formed in the jagged rocks.
A wave broke over her as she tried to get her
foot out, but she was stuck.

This is ridiculous, she said to herself. If her
foot had slipped in, surely it must be able to
come out again, but no matter how she tried
to extract it, it remained stuck. She felt much
too foolish to call anyone, although she could
see Greg with the others far up on the beach.
Another wave rolled over, a stronger wave
this time, throwing her over with its strength
and then, as it pulled back to the ocean she
feared it would take it with her. But her foot,
now securely stuck in the rift between the
rocks, kept her moored.

Her fear began to mount. She reached down
and tried desperately to free her foot but now
the water was too deep. *How could it happen
so quickly!* Another wave or two and she would
drown. Laurie panicked. Her life would be
cut off forever.

"Hey, help me! I'm stuck! Please!" she cried,
but the group on the dry shore could not have
heard her, though she thought Greg stopped

for a moment as if he might have heard something. But the wind had changed and her voice was carried north.

Really frightened now, she cried out once more, but this time her voice was buried in a wave that crashed against the rocks and pummeled Laurie as though a thousand fists were punching and pushing her. Then her head must have struck a rock for the deep green and purple of the water turned to deep violet and black. She resisted, but the black enveloped her. She thought, *It's over, it's all over now.*

How long she remained within the blackness she could not tell, but she opened her eyes with wonder that she was still alive as she saw a wet greenness and then the cobalt blue of the sky. Her foot was being twisted and pulled, and if it was painful it also seemed very far away. She was being lifted and carried, then set down on a sandy beach.

"Are you all right? Laurie, talk. Are you all right now?"

She opened her eyes and saw Greg as he bent over her. Never had he appeared more concerned, and when she nodded to show she was all right but could not yet speak, she thought his eyes were filled with love. Was this so or was it the strange state into which her near-drowning had thrown her? What she knew was that it was a miracle to be alive and that when she came back to life she had opened her eyes to see the person she loved.

"Thank you," she whispered, for she could not really speak.

His lips quivered. "Thank God, you're all right. You must be freezing. Hey, does someone have a towel, a blanket?"

Now everyone was helping out, finding towels and an extra shirt, a dry sweater. After a while Laurie sat up and though her foot was sore, Mr. Andrews examined it and didn't think it was broken.

"You're a lucky girl," he said.

"I'm the luckiest girl in the world," she answered, laughing, but she thought that this time it was true. Greg helped her up and insisted on walking beside her all the way back to the camp. *Yes*, she thought, *I'm grateful. To be alive is good luck and to be with Greg is the best of fortune.* Their friends walked with them, and it did not matter too much that her foot ached and she felt the need to sleep. At that moment everything in life was precious, never more precious.

Thanks to her narrow escape, the most ordinary things suddenly became remarkable. Joining her friends for dinner, freshly caught fish fried over a campfire — which would have been a new experience in any case — now seemed particularly joyful. It amazed her that she could enjoy it all so much — her friends, the laughter, the stories, and finally, after dessert and mugs of hot chocolate, attempts at singing by the group. They may have failed, but the one person who had brought along his guitar and could sing induced a sweet silence in the others as they listened and gazed at the flames of the campfire and retreated to private dreams.

"I think we'd better get some more wood," Greg said after a while. "Alan and I piled lots of driftwood on the beach. Want to come with me, Laurie?"

"Of course," she said, getting up. Although her foot still hurt and she limped ever so slightly, she wanted to be with Greg. When they reached the beach, they sat on an old log that had been left there and looked up at the stars that twinkled brilliantly in a deep, velvety sky.

"Look at them! I never knew there were so many. It's never like this in Edgewood," Laurie said and then, becoming more personal, turned to Greg. "How can I thank you, Greg? You saved my life. You risked your own to do it. You must have known what a dreadful undertow there was."

"You saved my life, too, Laurie."

"I don't understand what you mean."

He took a deep breath as though what he was about to say was not easy. "It's not easy to say this, Laurie. It was all I could do to admit to myself that I was falling in love with you because I didn't want to fall in love with anyone. But when I saw that I might lose you, I knew the most important thing in the whole world was to save you. You are so dear to me."

He paused and she waited. Then he continued.

"I swore I would never fall in love again. I'd had my lesson, it seems very long ago now. That was my decision, to go it alone, not to trust anyone again. But I love you, Laurie, I love you so much."

"I love you, too. But you must have known it!"

Now that they had confessed their feelings they laughed with relief, then embraced each other for a long time, sealing their words with a kiss. Then Laurie pulled away.

"I still don't understand why you kept away so long. I never could figure it out. I thought most likely you were in love with Jean, you know, the girl with you in the pizza parlor."

"Jean? Me in love with Jean?" He laughed. "Jean's my sister and I do like her, particularly since I get to see her only on vacations when she's home from school. You thought I was in love with her?"

"What a relief! All that worrying for nothing. Was there someone else?"

"It's not easy to talk about. When we lived in Santa Cruz, and I was beginning high school, I fell in love for the first time. At least it seemed like love. She was full of high spirits, adventurous, daring, lots of fun. I thought she loved me, too, had every reason to think so. My first girl! And then, someone else came along, a football captain — would you believe it? — and she dropped me flat."

"I'm sorry. Well, not really sorry because then I wouldn't have met you. But it must have hurt."

"It was a blow in the solar plexus. I felt deceived and hurt and angry and doubtful, as if there were something wrong with me. But I promised myself I'd never be that vulnerable again. I'd never fall in love. So when I came here, it was a jolt for me to see you and recognize those feelings."

"You mean you noticed me before we ever went jogging together?"

"Of course. Everyone knew you were going with Bob, and I figured you were part of the Gang and maybe just interested in parties."

"But it wasn't right for me. I never really belonged."

"I couldn't tell. It shocked me to see you in Pete's that night of the Christmas Dance and I began to think, hey, maybe I was wrong about you. And then when I saw you jogging . . ."

"What did you think then?"

He laughed quietly. "I thought you were probably the worst jogger I'd ever seen, but then I changed my mind. You're not so bad."

"Thank you very much." Laurie laughed.

"I was afraid to get too happy about seeing you every day. I kept wishing you would invite me to your house for breakfast or to meet your parents."

"Greg, it's exactly what I wanted to do! But you were so abrupt, I was afraid."

"Then I watched you. I became a 'Lauriewatcher.' Singing, running, the great paper you wrote, the way you wanted to go hiking. It was so great, but until today I didn't dare to tell you. Laurie, am I talking too much?"

She kissed him for an answer. Words were no longer necessary as they clung to each other. The waves of the ocean boomed as if applauding and the stars gleamed more brightly than they thought possible.

"I love you," Greg said. "It's so wonderful to be able to tell you."

Laurie murmured in agreement.

"I could stay on the beach all night like this," she told Greg, "but they'll be wondering about us back there. Aren't we supposed to be gathering driftwood?"

One more lingering kiss, and then they filled their arms with driftwood and walked back to the camp.